DEATH STALKS THE DIAMOND VALLEY

A TERRENCE CORCORAN WESTERN

JOHNNY GUNN

WOLFPACK
PUBLISHING
— EST 2013 —

WOLFPACK
PUBLISHING
— EST 2013 —

Published in the United States by Wolfpack Publishing, Las Vegas

Wolfpack Publishing
6032 Wheat Penny Avenue
Las Vegas, NV 89122

wolfpackpublishing.com

Paperback ISBN 978-1-64119-752-6
eBook ISBN 978-1-64119-751-9

DEATH STALKS THE DIAMOND VALLEY

CHAPTER ONE

"How high is that mountain, anyway?"

"Pretty near ten thousand feet, according to George Acres. He's been to the top twice."

"We gotta go clear to the top?"

"If the fool wearing the boots making the prints we're following goes that high." Sheriff Ed Connor and his deputy, Ed Lindstrom, were climbing toward Diamond Peak, north of Eureka, Nevada, on a cold November morning. Two renegade Shoshone Indians from the nearby reservation had slaughtered a calf and eaten some, smoked some, and gave away some. It wasn't their calf, and Connors and Lindstrom had chased the two to the Diamond Range.

"Should of shot both of 'em, Lindstrom, but since we didn't, we gotta chase this one down. Can't let them fools get away with this kind of nonsense. Killin' a calf just cuz it was there. Damn."

The Diamond Valley, north and west of Eureka, was lush cattle country, Eureka was the county seat of Eureka County, and the ranchers had been complaining loud and clear about rustling activity for months. Ranches up and down the valley summered their herds in the high range, finding good forage and plenty of water. More than one gang had found those herds rather easy pickings.

Sometimes, instead of a gang of rustlers, it would be one family or one small group simply looking for good beef. Those were the hardest to catch. In this case, Deputy Lindstrom had just happened onto the two men with what was left of the calf, and part of what was left was the hide with the brand fully evident.

Lindstrom had his revolver out quickly. "Gotta take you boys in. Killin' cows that don't belong to you might even get you hung," Lindstrom said. Neither man had a weapon and Lindstrom told them to turn around so he could cuff them. Instead, one whirled and kicked the gun out of the deputy's hand. The other grabbed a rock and smashed it into Ed Lindstrom's head, knocking him to the ground.

The two Shoshone men ran for their horses, and Lindstrom, dizzy and hurt, rolled through the mud toward his weapon. He managed to shoot one of them as they fled. His shot went deep into the man's hip, knocking him to the ground. Lindstrom got iron cuffs on the Shoshone outlaw and doctored the wound enough to get him in the saddle.

"One wrong move, amigo, and I'll drag your putrid body through the streets." The Indian never said a word as Linstrom doctored him or when he helped him into the saddle. Lindstrom took the time to doctor his own self, stopped the bleeding from the wound to his head, and mounted up.

"On the other hand, amigo, it will be a lot easier if you do try to escape. Lot's less paperwork and trouble." He gathered up the lead rope from his hostage's horse and then made his way back to town to put together a posse. Deputies Terrence Corcoran and Henry Carter were on a chase far north of town, and that just left the sheriff. Connor was a big man, enjoyed the job, kept a tight rein on the peace, and wasn't in the best of shape.

"You okay to make the ride? Your head looks like hell." Connor said what was on his mind, never mincing his words.

"I'm fine, Sheriff. Lookin' forward to kicking some Indian butt." Lindstrom was young, mean, and in fine physical shape despite what his head looked like at the moment. "Those two been causin' more trouble than the whole rest of the Shoshone Nation." They left out of town with short rations and high expectations. It wasn't hard to pick up the trail of the renegade and follow it into the high country. It wasn't long and they were into the snow, deep enough that they decided to leave the horses tied off.

"He's getting himself up into the heavy snow, Sheriff. We ain't had the least bit of break in the weather yet." They were on foot, fighting snow that was about one to three feet deep and only a few hundred feet above the valley floor. "He's sure to bunker up. Think he knows we're on his trail?"

Connor let out a yelp and collapsed to the ground before the gunshot was heard. Blood arced into the snow, and Lindstrom fell next to the sheriff, pulled his kerchief off and tied off Connor's leg, stemming the heavy flow. "Guess that's your answer," Conner coughed. "I'll take care of the leg. Kill that damned fool."

Lindstrom knew better than to argue and snaked his way through rocks and timber, trying to see where the Indian might be. "Has to be a ways off," he murmured. "Didn't hear the shot until Ed was down," he murmured, squirming through the snow-covered brush. It was steep and rough country, and now even more difficult because of the snow and ice.

The Diamond Range was excellent game country, filled with mule deer and elk, with antelope in the lower foothills and out through the valley. As were most of Nevada's ranges, the Diamond's run north and south was steep and rocky. The Western Shoshone had lived in this country for hundreds of generations and had an intimate knowledge of the terrain.

"I know who I'm chasing," Lindstrom muttered, "and I'm gonna make him pay for bashing my head, killing that steer, and shooting old Ed Connor." He got behind an outcrop, trying to spot some kind of movement. "Must be a ways out and a fine shooter. Bullet hit well before we heard the shot." He couldn't get that thought out of his head. "Some kind of shot, marksman all the way." He moved up, staying as low as possible, using tall pine trees and boulders for cover, and was about to move again when he spotted the man.

"So, you're just gonna sit there and wait for me, eh? Ain't so, Mr. Cattle Rustler, ain't so." He muttered the whole time he brought the rifle to his shoulder and only stopped to take a long and careful aim. The Winchester belched smoke and fire, the Indian screamed and jumped to his feet, and the Winchester spoke a second time. It was then quiet.

"Ain't this just dandy," Lindstrom said. "Got a dead Indian, a wounded sheriff, and our horses are two miles downhill. Well, just damn me." He decided to leave the rustler's body where it was but gathered up all the weapons. He knew there wasn't anyone else, and decided to go back to help Connor get back to the horses. "We'll just leave you there, buddy. You cain't be in any worse shape," he said to the dead Indian.

Lindstrom took one look at Sheriff Connor's leg and let go a stream of vulgarities that hadn't been heard in those mountains in years. "Ed, I gotta let you be for a bit. That bone is broke clear through and comin' out your pants leg. I can't carry you off this mountain. Gotta get the horses. Don't try to do anything dumb while I'm gone."

"Not me. You just hurry, Mr. Lindstrom." He tried to smile and Lindstrom had to turn aside. Enough time had gone by that the initial pain was replaced by the hard pain and ache of broken bones and ripped flesh. Connor wasn't that strong, spent too much time at his desk, and was fighting the pain. Lindstrom could see that the sheriff was getting weak from loss of blood.

"What a dumb-ass time to not have anyone with us," the deputy muttered, making his way through the heavy snow back to their horses. "Shoulda made one of those fellers at the bar come with us. Ed's just too easy going sometimes." Between some strong cussing and heavy breathing, the two miles slipped by.

It was a hard ride back up, and Lindstrom was afraid he'd find a dead sheriff when he got there. Connor was unconscious but not dead, and he had managed to get most of the heavy bleeding stopped. "You're gonna be a mess by the time I get you back to town," the deputy said. "Don't even know how I'm gonna get you on that horse."

He got the sheriff awake enough that he could help and boosted the big man into the saddle. "Don't be puttin' no weight on that leg," Lindstrom said. It was dark late in the evening when they finally started down the long trail. "Gonna be blacker'n a coon's head before we get to town, Ed, so just hang on tight."

Connor may have been older, more out of shape than his deputy, but no one ever questioned his being one tough hombre. It wasn't that long ago many could remember Ed Connor taking on two at a time in more than one saloon fight. "We'll make it, Lindstrom," he said. "We'll make it. Just get me to Doc Weatherford's and then find Corcoran. We'll make it."

Ed Lindstrom wasn't that sure of it, he could feel the wind picking up and knew they would be fighting bitter cold before hitting town. It was a slow trip off the mountain, and Lindstrom followed the railroad tracks back to the little community of Eureka. Doc Weatherford was already in his cups and cussed up a storm when Lindstrom half carried, half dragged the sheriff into his home.

"Rifle shot, Doc. Lost a lot of blood. Gotta go find Corcoran," the deputy said, getting Connor laid out on a long wooden table.

"Help me get his boots and pants off and you can go anywhere you want, Deputy. Where'd this happen?"

"About halfway up Diamond Peak. Indian rustler. But not no more," Lindstrom chuckled. "Before I leave, have you got something for this headache of mine. Bastards whupped me with a rock."

Weatherford made Lindstrom sit down, cleaned the wound and dressed it, then gave him something harsh to drink. "That's horrible," Lindstrom said. "It better work cuz I sure ain't askin' for seconds."

"Don't like it, don't drink it. Brandy's better anyway," the cagey old doc laughed, shooing the young deputy out. "Bonanza's got some good brandy. Designed for young men with bashed-in heads."

Lindstrom didn't know whether to laugh or cuss, si he just walked out, knowing the first stop would be the Bonanza Club.

CHAPTER TWO

Ed Lindstrom made his way, instead, to the sheriff's office and found Corcoran and part-time Deputy Henry Carter sitting near a red-hot, potbelly stove, drinking coffee. "Got a problem, Corcoran," he said. He poured himself a cup and settled in at the sheriff's desk.

"Lookin' at your head, I'd say that's an understatement," Corcoran chuckled. "What've you been up to?"

"Ed's been shot bad. He's at the doc's and wants to see you. Doc's in a twit, too."

"Course he is," Corcoran said. "It's after five. It's his drinkin' time. What happened to Connor? You don't look too good yourself. Sit down and tell me all about it."

Lindstrom told his tale and Corcoran jumped up to high-tail it to Doc Weatherford's. "These Indians part of a rustling gang?" Corcoran had been fighting a gang for several weeks and couldn't get a handle on them.

"Don't think so. Dumb bastards. Slaughtered the animal and didn't get rid of the skin and brand. No, not a gang."

Terrence Corcoran was in his thirties, tall and rangy with a full head of long, wavy, reddish hair that hung to his shoulders. The girls loved to run their fingers through that hair while Corcoran's fingers did their little dance as well. He took off for the doc's, telling Henry Carver to go home to his kids.

Corcoran's as Irish as if he had been born on that little green jewel, but the truth is, he was born on a boat four days into its trip from the Emerald Isles to New York. He'd never stepped a foot on Irish soil, but he could talk the talk with the best of them.

"You look like hell, Connor," he said, standing next to the sheriff's bed. "Lindstrom said the two Shoshone are dead. Good job."

"He did it. Got both of them. The bullet busted my leg right in two, Terrence. I'm gonna be on my back for weeks, the doc says. He's got me in a cast from my toes to my chest, and ropes pulling on my feet. You're my chief deputy, Corcoran. You know damn well you should be sheriff, so for the next several weeks, you are."

"You and Carter bust up those rustlers you been

chasing?"

"Nope. We got most of the cattle back but not them. They knew we were coming, Ed, just like last time. I don't want to be sheriff, you know that. I'll keep your seat warm for you, but don't you even think about quitting. It took me a long time to get a man in that seat who's up to the job. Doc gonna keep you here?"

Sheriff Ed Connor lost his wife two years ago and lived alone in a big house on the east side of town, about a block off the main street. His son was a Texas Ranger and his daughter was a lawyer in San Francisco, so there wouldn't be anyone to care for a bedridden man.

"Doc's gonna keep me here until I can make arrangements. How the hell am I gonna do that?" The frustration of the situation was already setting in. Connor was a get-it-done kind of man, never asked for help unless it was absolutely necessary. "Can't even take a piss without help." He cussed some and then chortled some but there was also fear in his eyes, a fear that maybe this wouldn't end well at all, that maybe his days of being fully capable of taking care of himself were coming to a close.

No man wanted that kind of fear, particularly a man who rarely asked for help. "Don't laugh about this, Corcoran. It's serious. What if that leg don't heal up right? What if I can't do my job, take care of myself?" Corcoran had never seen this side of the man. He always saw the strong, get-er-done Ed Connor and wasn't really sure what to say.

"I'll swing by Angie's," Corcoran said. "A couple of her girls have always had a crush on you."

"Don't you dare," Connor bellowed. "No, no, no," he said. "I'll fire you," he threatened, and Corcoran laughed right out. "I will. I swear, Corcoran. Don't you bring one of those doves around."

Corcoran was still laughing as he made his way from Doc Weatherford's and down the street to the Bonanza Club. *You ain't gonna like it old man, but those girls would take better care of you than anyone ever has. Damn me, but this is a bad time for you to get shot, with rustlers running around like we ain't even here, and shorthanded too.* He was right, though. *I always say I don't want to be sheriff, just being a deputy is my call in life, but I do want to be sheriff. But only I know that.*

"Corcoran," she howled, running from the kitchen and throwing herself in his arms. "I heard about the shooting and thought it was you. Oh, God, I'm glad you're safe." Little, skinny Cindy Payton, cook, sometimes barmaid, in love with Corcoran, had tears running down her cheeks, hugging the big man as tight as possible.

"You know I wouldn't let myself get shot and make you all worried," he joked, easing her feet back to the floor. "Ed Connor got shot, though, bad. Jimmy around tonight?" He gave her bottom a quick pat, ducked the right cross, and laughed some.

"Oh, you're a dickens, Terrence Corcoran." She loved the little love pats but always took a quick and soft swing at the big man.

Jimmy was Jimmy Henderson, owner of the Bonanza Club. When gold was discovered near the canyon, Henderson put up a tent saloon and called it his bonanza. It'd grown into a two-story business that included a saloon and gambling hall, restaurant, and hotel, and had been a bonanza in every sense of the word.

"He's upstairs with Mr. Bridges," she said. "They've been talking for a long time."

Corcoran gave her another quick little pat on her cute bottom, got a swat in return, and headed up the grand staircase to Henderson's offices. "Must have chopped down five oak trees just to panel the office and make the desk," he scoffed, often. Henderson didn't pay him no mind, he'd tell anyone who'd listen. The carpet was wool, there were brocade drapes hung with velvet and silk adornments, and a chandelier fitted out with the finest crystal.

Henderson lived high from his 'Bonanza' and want-ed everyone to know it. "You don't see those mining nabobs hiding from their good luck, do you? Damn right, I'm not going to," he'd laugh loud and offer a fine Virginia cigar or a belt of California brandy. "I was in the right place at the right time and I'm loving it."

On the other hand, if someone in the county fell on hard times, Jimmy Henderson was right there. If the county couldn't afford something Henderson ap-proved of, the money showed up. He wasn't a true soft touch, he expected to get paid back but never pressed the subject either.

At any time, one would find buckaroos from ranches up and down the Diamond Valley, or miners from one or more of the producing mines that created Eureka, or those involved in transportation or other commerce at the saloon's long oaken planks and gambling tables. The Bonanza Club was the hub of social life in Eureka.

Live music was provided by a small band of a banjo, piano, and harmonica, with a fiddle player jumping in if around. The cocktail girls were always available for dancing, and some of them, for other pleasures.

"Evening Jimmy, Bridges. Need to talk with both of you," Corcoran said, easing into a large, wing-back chair near a blazing fireplace.

"Corcoran," Peter Bridges said. "Good, because we need to talk with you. Brandy?"

Bridges owned the Eureka Bank, was somewhere in his fifties, tough as a sun-dried cob, armed all his employees and gave them orders to kill anyone attempting to rob his bank. He smoked huge cigars, drank copious amounts of brandy and whiskey, and took part in the July Fourth wrestling matches, putting more than one buckaroo or miner on the sick list.

"I keep hearing rumors of a gang of outlaws moving into our territory, Corcoran. You know anything about that?" He poured a generous snifter full for the deputy.

"I've been thinking on that, Bridges. A gang of rustlers has been moving through the Diamond Valley, and these men aren't just taking a few steers at a time. That may not be what you're talking about, though."

"No, not rustlers, Terrence, bank robbers, train robbers." Bridges sat back, took a long drag on his cigar, to see Corcoran's reaction. "These mines of ours send their gold to the mints and other markets on the trains and I get my money from the mints by way of the trains. Bank robbers stay away from the Central Pacific, but I'm not sure they will stay away from our spur line."

"I've heard those same rumors," Corcoran said. "Most outlaws know how you feel about bank-robbing," he chuckled, "and stay away from your bank. The trains are a different subject. What about you, Jimmy? They coming to hit the Bonanza Club?"

"Only if they want to die," Henderson snarled. "But the rumors are out there. You said you had something for us, Terrence?"

"Yup, and it ain't good. Ed Connor got shot up earlier today and will be laid up for several weeks. He wants me to run the office. We're already shorthanded. Anyone in town good enough to wear a Eureka County badge?"

"You might want to talk to George Acres at the feed store. He keeps pretty close eye on the comings and goings around town," Bridges said.

"Wrong time of the year to be hiring, Corcoran," Henderson said. "Mines have gobbled up anyone out of work for the winter. You gonna put Carter on full-time?"

"I need two full-time deputies and Carter won't be one of them. Something wrong with that boy. I'm not sure I trust him." Corcoran took another offering of brandy from Peter Bridges and lit a cigar. "Think I'll wander over to Sandy McAuliff's hovel," he chuckled. "Maybe even pin a badge on the old coot."

"Wouldn't be the first time he's worn one," Bridges said. "I don't want to hound on the subject, but the idea of a gang moving into the area, bothers me. Not just the bank, mind you, but the community. We have built our little mining camp into a nice town, good families, strong economy. Find this gang, Corcoran."

Corcoran felt the pressure and understood where it was coming from. Ranchers up and down the rich little valley fighting off rustlers and now businessmen in town frightened of a possible gang moving in. "I'm ready for this fight, Bridges," he said, drank his brandy down and slipped out of the office.

"That ain't good, Connor all shot up." Bridges flicked ash from his cigar and walked around the room. "Is Corcoran up to that job? Full-time Sheriff? I know he's tough as iron, but is as smart as he is tough?"

"I'd bet on it, Bridges. Tried to talk him into running for the job more than once. He's smart, Bridges, you can bank on it."

"I am."

CHAPTER THREE

Five men sat around the stove, in a cabin far back in a deep canyon in the Diamond Range. The one-room cabin was built of aspen logs felled in the glade and was abandoned years ago. It was often used by hunters and prospectors. The men were listening to Colonel Buford S. Cornell, supposedly a civil war veteran and more locally known as a heavy drinker. Colonel Cornell passed himself off as a war veteran and an expert on almost any subject that came to hand.

He could and would tell you why the train might be late. How best to protect your herd from rustlers, or, if the conversation went the other way, how best to rustle that herd. He was an expert on protecting a bank one day, and how to rob a bank the next day. Robbing banks seemed to be a specialty of his and he insisted that he knew how to rob the Eureka Bank.

"You was asking me about that bank, Dupree," Cornell said. "It's a fortress. Old Bridges built it out of rocks and steel, has all his employees armed at all times, and carries a ten gauge double barrel himself. I had thoughts about that bank myself when I first moved here, and haven't given up the idea. Fact is, I have a plan." His long, white, wavy hair spilled down his back and across his shoulders, and when he spoke his white mustache and goatee quivered as if his talk was supposed to mean something. The astute among the group saw a man in love with himself.

"That's the way Silas Arnold described it," Clarence Dupree said.

"You know Arnold? He was a rustler, worked the Diamond Valley a few years ago. How is it you know Silas Arnold." Colonel Cornell shook his head.

"Served time together," was all Dupree said.

Cornell always tucked his breeches into his high boots, wore a buckskin jacket fitted out with fringes and beaded decorations, carried a military holster for his Colt on one side, and a long Bowie knife on the other. The only thing he never bragged about was riding with Custer.

"Arnold was a mean one. His brother was a half-wit."

"Yeah, Colonel, I've been called mean, too. Don't

want to forget that." Dupree was a mean man, angry most of the time, never satisfied with how others handled their jobs or life. Near thirty, his little gang had moved west from Denver, working its way toward what they considered the big time of San Francisco. The possibility of hitting the Eureka Bank had been brought to their attention by the rustler Arnold. Dupree heard about Cornell from Arnold and they came to check out this rich little bank.

Vicious killers all, some were not run of the mill outlaws. They did well on the outlaw trail, had money to burn, dressed well, had good taste in food and drink.

Jimmy the Cueball, Joey Kinkaid, and Oscar Owens made up the rest of the gang. It was Owens who had most of the brains, the Cueball was a born killer, sinfully stupid, and Kinkaid wanted to be the leader but feared Dupree. Col. Cornell wasn't a part of the gang, but his bluster around town about guns, battles, knowledge of banks and schedules, brought him to this point.

"It's like I said from the start, Dupree," Owens said. "The money we want isn't in the bank, it's on one of those train cars coming in. The Eureka and Palisades connects with the Western Pacific and the bank's money arrives in an armored coach. The mines send their gold out the same way." It was Owens' meeting with Cornell after Arnold told Dupree about him that brought the gang to Eureka and the railroad that made it worth the trip.

"I remember, it was Richmond, during the big war, we blew up half a dozen trains trying to get Union money," Col. Cornell said for no reason whatever.

"I thought you were a bluebelly," Kinkaid said.

"Did I say union money? I meant Reb money," Cornell said, quickly. Which side was the man really on? Was he even there? Dupree had enough.

"Thank you for your help, Colonel," Dupree said. He was exasperated, having been told that this colonel was supposed to be some kind of expert about banks. "We'll let you know if we need any more of your help." He handed the colonel a gold eagle and escorted him from the cabin.

"Damn blow-hard fool," he muttered, coming back. "How do we get the railroad schedules? Coming and going." He paced around the table, stopped for a shot of whiskey, and looked at Owens. "You've been all over that town for a week, Oscar. What're your ideas?"

"Been making friends with a kid who works at the bank. Name's Johnny Lewis. Dumb as dirt but knows all the schedules of the trains, the employees, even when old man Bridges does his duty," he laughed. "I'll keep working on him and get it down. We'll need dynamite and wrecking tools for the coaches. Those doors usually lock from the inside so we can't just blow the lock off."

"We have a friend in the sheriff's office, too," Kinkaid said. "Met him in the saloon the other night. He only works part-time. He has a proud mouth," he sneered. "A couple of shots of whiskey and he talks his fool head off. There's a deputy we'll have to watch out for. Name's Corcoran, Terrence Corcoran. Supposed to be some kind of hotshot lawman."

"Those are the kind I like to kill," Jimmy the Cueball chuckled. "So, what's the plan, Dupree?"

Dupree glanced at Oscar Owens, stood up and moved around the little cabin putting all this information together. They had come west robbing banks, knew how to rob banks, and this idea of holding up trains didn't sit that well. Still, if that Bank of Eureka was really a fortress, then the idea of getting the money before it reached the bank was a good one.

"Owens, get all the information you can on schedules, Kinkaid, get close to that deputy, and Cueball, you and me will gather dynamite and tools. After the jobs in Cheyenne and Salt Lake, there might be paper out on us, gentlemen, so let's not know each other when we're in town. We'll meet back here in three days."

It was late in the afternoon as Oscar Owens and

Joey Kinkaid rode off for Eureka. "You have a room, Joey?"

"No, don't want one. Got a little camp in the canyon east of town. Hidden back in the trees. That Mexican jail made me so I hate walls. Get all jumpy when I'm corralled like that."

"I'm staying at the Bonanza, so we better not ride in together. We'll split off when we get to the railhead. How'd you come to meet that deputy?"

"He just come up to the bar and was telling the barman about the sheriff getting shot. I kinda got into the talk, is all."

"The sheriff was shot? When?"

"Must have been yesterday or the day before. Laid up for weeks, Carter said. This feller Corcoran is acting sheriff now."

"Damn," Owens said. "You didn't think that was important enough to tell Dupree?" Owens was furious at the kid. "They ain't no full-time sheriff, just an acting one, and we're planning to rob trains and you didn't mention that? Damn."

"Go to hell, Owens. Don't get in my craw. I'll tell him when we meet. He'll probably know by then, anyway. I don't like the way you talk to me. You better be careful about how you talk to me," Kinkaid said, and rode off toward Eureka at a lope, leaving Owens in a cloud of angry dust.

"Damn fool kid," Owens said. "I better do some digging when I get to town. Wonder what else he knows that he didn't tell us. Like maybe the trains won't be running or something. I hate kids." Kinkaid was maybe twenty, said he had killed six, said he escaped from that Mexican jail. "Never have seen paper on him, though," Owens muttered.

Corcoran was sitting at his desk with Ed Lindstrom and Henry Carter in chairs by the stove. It was a cold morning and most were sure a storm was on its way. "I talked with Sandy McAuliff and George Acres the other day and both recommended Amos White for the open deputy position. He'll be here in a few minutes. Anyone else you can think of? We need at least one more man."

"I'd like to be a ful- time deputy," Henry Carter said.

"You know you can't be," Corcoran snuffed. "You ain't married and have two kids. You got a store to tend to, and you got an old mother you take care of. Ain't enough hours left over, Henry. We've been through all this before. And don't get angry and stomp out again, either. That's getting old."

Carter stood up, thought better of it, and sat back

down. "I could make it work," he muttered.

"What's the need for this second deputy?" Ed Lindstrom asked. "You, me, and White could cover the town pretty good."

"I'd like to have a jailer," Corcoran said. "These rumors of a gang working those rustling jobs, and threats to the bank, if they're true, will stretch us too thin. Come on now, one more name."

Before anyone could answer, Amos White walked in. Tall, heavy, iron-tough, and with a youthful grin on his face. "Afternoon, Corcoran. Howdy, Lindstrom." He offered his hand to Corcoran and took a chair by the stove. "Hello, Carter, didn't expect to see you here."

"Why not? I am a deputy."

"Part-time," Ed Lindstrom snarled. "Nice to see you, Amos, and your muscles, and your big guns." He wore a Colt on his side and carried a double barrel shotgun he filched from a stage messenger a few years ago. "You got a horse big enough to carry you and your guns?"

Only Carter wasn't laughing. "Have some coffee, White, and I'll bring you up to date on what's going on around this old camp. Ed, make your rounds and keep your ears open."

"What about me?" Henry Carter asked.

"Take care of your store and your kids, Henry. We'll call out if we need you."

He scraped the chair hard getting up and stomped out the door, muttering some nasty words on the way.

"Man doesn't understand what it means to be a lawman," Corcoran said. "It's all day every day, all night every night. Not just when it's convenient. Well, now, Mr. White, let's talk about you. We might have some bad stuff coming our way and we need help."

"I'm twenty-two, raised on a ranch, worked laying rail for awhile, but always wanted to wear a badge. Oh, and, I ain't married, got no kids, and my ma died years ago."

"And you want to be one of us because the girls love a man with a badge?" Corcoran laughed.

"Ain't nothing wrong with that," Amos White chuckled, "but because there are too many people breaking the laws and making life dangerous for those that work hard for a living. Sounds kind of uppity, I guess, but that's the way I feel." He had embarrassed himself in front of this monster of a deputy and tried to hide it. Put Mr. White and Mr. Corcoran together and the five hundred pound marker would be threatened.

"That's pretty much the way I feel too, Mr. White," Corcoran said. "I think we'll get along just fine. Ed Connor is the sheriff, I'm just standing in for a while, so let's you and me walk over there and get you sworn in."

White carried a wide smile the whole walk to Ed Connor's large, ranch-style home. Maryann Soto let them in. "Miss Soto's taking care of the sheriff until he gets back on his feet," Corcoran said. He got a big hug and peck on the cheek from the charming lady. "Yup, Amos, pretty girls do like a man wearing a badge."

Maryann Soto spent more time hustling drinks and helping gamblers lose their money at the Bonanza Club than she did nursing sick sheriffs, but this job was different. Jimmy Henderson promised her job back when Ed Connor got back on his feet, and the county promised to pay her a handsome sum to take care of the sheriff. Besides that, she had a crush on the crusty gentleman.

"He's still in a foul mood, Terrence," she warned as he walked toward the bedroom door. "He might throw something."

Corcoran beat his fist against the door and hollered, "You in there Ed? The whole Sioux Nation is coming down on us," and he beat on the door again. That brought some bellowing then some genuine laughter, and Corcoran snuck through the door. "Well, now, just look at you."

Connor was stretched out, a cast running down his right side from just below his waist to his foot, and it was strung up with weights pulling on the leg. "Help me figure how to get out of this mess, Corcoran or so help me ..." and it trailed off. "Who's that with you?"

"Meet Amos White. I want him to be a deputy if you'll do the honors. Come on in here, Amos and say howdy to the boss of the county."

"It's my pleasure, Sheriff. Always been a supporter of yours."

"That's the way," Connor said. "Soft butter for the boss. You are big enough. You tough and mean, like Corcoran here?"

"That might be a stretch, Sheriff," he chuckled.

"Honesty always works with me," Connor said. He had White raise his hand and swore him in. Corcoran pulled a badge from his vest and pinned it on him. "What's the word around town, Corcoran, they gonna throw me out?"

"No, Ed, ain't no one gonna throw you out. Peter Bridges is sure his bank is gonna get hit, and Jimmy Henderson has the same thoughts about the Bonanza Club. Rumors of a gang in the area are the hot topic. That's why I wanted White in here with us. His size alone would scare off Farmer Peas."

Maryanne stuck her head in. "Got a visitor, Sheriff. You up to it?" He nodded and she turned and brought Peter Bridges into the almost crowded bedroom.

"Can't protect my bank if the whole department is in here drinkin' and carousin'," he snarled, but Corcoran caught the sly grin. "Desperadoes out there, Connor, what are you doin' in bed?"

"Hello, Pete. Corcoran was just telling me about your thoughts. What gives you the idea there might be a hit on your bank?"

"Couple of people come in asking about opening an account, looking at everything, but not opening an account. They were looking at my defenses, Ed, sure as hell. I wrote down what I thought they looked like for you," he said. He pulled a couple of pieces of paper from his frock coat and handed them to Corcoran. "Seen these two?"

Corcoran read the sheets and handed them to Amos White. "Don't think so but sure will be on the look out for them. How about you, Amos?"

"This one, young, skinny, thin scraggly beard has been hanging around the Bonanza Club late in the evening, I think. Calls himself Joey. Might want to talk to Carter about him. Carter closes his shop and goes to the bar every night. He's been talking with this Joey feller."

"It's time for you gentlemen to leave now," Maryann Soto said. "The sheriff needs his lunch and Doctor Weatherford will be here shortly as well." Ed Connor had to smile, caught Corcoran giving him an evil grin, and then tried to growl his disfavor. The three men walked out onto a blustery street.

"Storm's a comin'," Bridges said. "In more ways than one. Keep me on your shortlist, Corcoran." Bridges headed down the hill toward his bank.

"Find Ed Lindstrom, White, and stay close to him. He'll give you the whole rundown on how we run things. Remember, you're the face of Eureka County in many eyes. Most know you're there to keep them safe, it's only a few that get stupid. Tell Ed you can find me either at the Bonanza Club or down at Sandy McAuliff's."

Interesting that Carter would be talking to a stranger in the evenings but not say anything about it at our meeting. He doesn't have it in him to be a lawman. The instinct of a lawman is to see a conspiracy in everything, to suspect everyone, particularly strangers, of having criminal intent. Corcoran had a smile on his face walking the dirt streets of Eureka even if the wind had a nasty bite to it.

When he first rode through, the street was lined with tents, he remembered. Corcoran spent his early law enforcement years in Virginia City but a visit to Eureka after an unfortunate experience on the Comstock, and he knew he wanted to live here. "Damn cold in the winter and not too hot in the summer makes, it nice," he muttered.

CHAPTER FOUR

"Sandy, you in there? It's Corcoran. Don't shoot," he hollered. Sandy McAuliff was in his late fifties or more, had tracked for the army, but most recently had tracked for Corcoran when he chased down a gang of killers. He considered himself an older man, wore a full red beard, and his long, red hair was braided and hanging down his back. He'd carve out a pipe and smoked it until no more smoke could get through the stem, and carve out a new one, drank his whiskey straight, no ice.

"Ha! Didn't even see me when you passed me by, did you, youngster," he cackled. He stepped out from a rose hedge, his shotgun in hand. "You're gettin' sloppy hanging around town all day and night, Corcoran."

"Might be at that, old man. Got some good whiskey from your home country? We need to talk."

"Sure and ya know it, Irish. Come on in, the fire's

hot, and this wind's got a curse to it. You want to know about that feller Joey who's been chattin' up your deputy, do ya?"

"And how long have you known about that, McAuliff?" They sat in comfortable chairs near the fireplace in McAuliff's tiny little cabin, sipping twelve-year-old Scotch whiskey. "Peter Bridges fears a gang is around to bust up his bank."

"Don't know about a gang but there have been strangers about recently. This Joey being one of them. He's a young kid, dresses well but wants to give off the appearance of being a tough guy. Saw plenty of them types in the army. Most of 'em second lieutenants," he chortled. "By the way, have you met the new girl Jimmy Henderson hired? Whooooie," he hollered.

Corcoran, laughing, said, "No but you're gonna tell me all about her, ain't you?"

"We'll walk down and meet her. What I did want to tell you, though was that Colonel Cornell has been blustering about some fellers he met that came in from Salt Lake recently. Don't know if this Joey is one of them, but Cornell said one of them was named Dupree and another Owens. Mean anything to you?"

"Dupree? We just got a poster on a man named Dupree. Not a common name." He was trying to remember what those posters said, what the crimes were, and tossed the rest of the whiskey down. "What did our good colonel have to say?"

"He talks in circles and rarely says anything that means anything. Don't have any idea how he gets involved in these things, but he seems to think this Dupree might be here to start a new banking operation."

"Or rob an existing one," Corcoran chuckled. "Buford Cornell's ability to tell the truth is seriously lacking, Sandy. One conversation finds him fighting for the Union, and the next, fighting for the rebs. Other than those names, did he say anything useful?"

"Only thing I got out of any of it was he kept bringing up banks, the Eureka Bank in particular, and that he might be involved when it all comes together, whatever 'it' is," McAuliff said.

"Gotta get back to the office and find those posters, Sandy. I'll meet you at the Bonanza Club in a few. Find a table by the windows." Corcoran had gangs, bank robbers, and danger racing through his mind as he made his way back to the office. *Cornell might be working with this gang that I keep hearing about and not even realize it. So stupid he'll probably end up being the leader.*

Corcoran couldn't help but remember that it was Colonel Cornell who constantly reminded all what an expert at banks he was. How he had robbed banks during the war for one side or the other, how he could simply walk through a bank and be able to rob it at will. *Damn blowhard is gonna get someone killed with his wild nonsense.*

The poster he wanted was near the top of a large stack on the sheriff's desk. "Clarence Dupree, wanted for murder and bank robbery in Salt Lake City," Corcoran murmured. "Two others with him, and these must be their posters. Joseph Kinkaid and Oscar Owens." His muttering continued for several minutes. "No pictures, damn it. Just descriptions. Kinkaid very young, scraggly beard, and long thin hair. Dresses well. That matches with what McAuliff said.

"This Owens is older and with nothing to make him stand out. Dupree is short and very heavy. Not fat, though. I should be able to spot two out of the three," he chuckled and brought the posters along with him to the Bonanza Club. He had not forgotten that Henderson had hired a new girl for the club. *I wonder if old Sandy McAuliff might want to wear a badge again and be my jailer? He sure done good for me on that long ride we made.*

The wind had picked up, the clouds were moving through the high mountain skies at a brisk rate, and Corcoran could almost smell the promise of snow by morning. "Too early for winter. Comes earlier and earlier every year, it seems." People moving about had their heads tucked deep into heavy jackets, horses were skittery with blowing leaves and other debris, and he enjoyed the aroma of many wood fires warming the buildings and bungalows of town.

Eureka sits in a canyon at the southern end of the Diamond Mountains separating Diamond Valley from Long Valley, with a broad main street running east and west. That street hosted thousands of those traveling to the goldfields of California. Some of them stopped long enough in the canyon to get their pans out. Gold was discovered and so was Eureka.

It was a small mining camp when Corcoran made his first visit, on a long ride from here to there, he remembered, a smile crossing his rugged face. *I've had a good life, I have. Worked for some fine lawmen, worked for some who should never have been allowed to wear a badge. Connor was right, though. If I ever wanted to be the sheriff, it would be right here in Eureka.*

The Bonanza Club was filled with men getting out of the gathering storm and he spotted McAuliff at a table by the big window that looked out on the main street. Buckaroos from nearby ranches, miners off shift from the big mines, and townsfolk getting out of the storm, were in a party mood this cold evening. "Seems like more than half the town's here, Sandy,"

Corcoran said taking a chair. "Have you seen Ed Lindstrom? Need to talk to him. Thanks again for telling me about Amos White. Seems like a good man."

Before McAuliff could answer Betty Cord walked up to the table. At twenty-two, nearly six feet tall, wearing a skimpy dance hall outfit, the redhead had Corcoran's attention immediately. "My, my," he muttered. "Such a charming child." *I haven't seen legs that long since the last horse auction.* His eyes brightened, worked their way from her heels to the top of the lady's head, pausing a time or two. She did the same and they both wore smiles.

"This, old friend, is Betty Cord, recently of Virginia City. You two already have a bit in common," McAuliff said. The twinkle in his eyes could be seen by anyone. "Ease your mouth closed, Terrence, and say hello."

Corcoran jumped to his feet, ripped his hat off, showing his flowing dark red waves of hair. "Miss Cord. How do you do? I'm Corcoran, Terrence Corcoran, at your service."

Her green eyes sparkled with warmth and humor, and she gave the big deputy a quick curtsy. "I've been warned, Corcoran," she said. "You have a bit of a reputation in these parts, and I've heard stories of your exploits on the Comstock. You shot the sheriff?"

"And put him in prison. Yes," he said. "That's a sad

story we'll not retell. What brings you to Eureka? Not exactly a town filled with promise for a young lady."

"Oh, but it may be. I'm a seamstress, Mr. Corcoran, and I lost just about everything in a fire several months ago. I met Jimmy Henderson several months before that and he tried to persuade me to come work for him then. I plan to hustle enough drinks, and dance with enough charming men, to buy all new equipment and material, and reopen my business here."

"The lady has her eyes on the road, Mr. McAuliff," Corcoran chuckled. He turned back to Betty Cord and smiled. "I would certainly enjoy being one of those charming men you will be dancing with."

"I do hope so," she smiled back. "What are you drinking, Sheriff?"

"Acting Sheriff," he corrected. "Bring a pot of coffee and a bottle of brandy, dear Betty, and ask those two deputies of mine at the end of the bar to join me, please." He stood again, took her hand and kissed it gently, bowed slightly, and winked. The wink was returned with a smile.

"I have memories of lovely ladies, too," McAuliff said. He sat back with a sigh, his eyes following Betty Cord as she waltzed toward the bar. "There was a young lady in Saint Loo, once, who stole my heart and then took great delight in smashing it into a million pieces. She drove me west, Terrence, boy. It was because of Sylvia McAndrews that I learned the ways of the mountains."

"And because of her we get to listen to your many stories of Indians, soldiers, and failed relationships," Corcoran laughed, getting a serious glare from the old Scot.

"You'll go too far one day, Terrence. Aye, you will tempt the gods once too often."

Corcoran was laughing hard as Ed Lindstrom and Amos White came to the table with their beers and sat down. "I have some posters here, Ed, that I think you and Amos need to study hard. Chances are these men might be in town right now. Hear anything on your walk around town?"

Lindstrom had the posters opened up on the table and Amos White pointed out Joey Kinkaid's description. "That's the man who's been talking with Henry Carter, I'd bet my first paycheck. Don't recognize the others."

"Descriptions are too vague," Lindstrom said. "Put out a poster like this, there should be pictures or drawings. You are sure there's gonna be a robbery of some kind, aren't you, Corcoran? Let's hear your thoughts." Lindstrom's bruises were stark in their various shades of purple. He had been carrying a badge for enough years that Corcoran knew he would be a fine lawman for the rest of his life.

Corcoran spent the next half hour outlining what he thought might happen if there really was a gang looking to hit the small town. "Our fine Colonel Cornell might have a play in some of this, so it might all just be wild talk." He also wondered if there might be two operations. One bunch going for the bank and another gang of outlaws rustling. Or, was there a connection?

"We know for a fact there is a rustling gang well established in the Diamond Valley. They seem to know who is moving cattle and when to strike. Inside information from someone. It would be scary to think that same gang is planning to raid our bank."

"It would be unusual," McAuliff said. He was scowling as he looked around the busy saloon. "They may all be outlaws, but there's a big difference between a bank robber and a cattle rustler. I'd put my money on two distinct operations," the old tracker said.

It was late when Jimmy the Cueball rode back into town. He and Dupree had lined up boxes of dynamite, fuse, and blasting caps, and had them hidden in the cabin in the mountains. Dupree was going to stay at the cabin and Cueball wanted a steak and whiskey, maybe some rough time with a woman. He hated most women, his mother in particular. Beating them into submission was far better than the act of sex itself.

If Jimmy had a last name he didn't know what it was, nor did he care. The first twelve years of his life with his mother were a living hell in his mind, with one man after another sharing space. The skinny little kid was beaten by them, by his mother, by anyone who needed to beat on somebody who couldn't fight back. The helpless kid was filled with hate and one night it exploded when a drunken freighter beat him bloody and passed out next to his mother.

Jimmy took the man's weapon and fired three shots into his head, then three shots into his mother's. He reloaded the Colt, tucked it in his waist, grabbed the man's poke, and never looked back. There has been a list of bruised and bloody women and dead men all along the trail left by Jimmy the Cueball. He was just twenty-three or so when he lost all his hair following a severe fever, thus the name.

He honed his ability with a handgun, was deadly with a rifle, and never balked at fighting a man with his knife. He loved to kill almost as much as he loved beating on women. Every woman looked just like his mother. He walked through the heavy front doors of the Bonanza Club and up to the bar. "Whiskey, Barman, and a clean glass." The saloon and restaurant were full-on what was sure to be a cold and stormy night in the canyon.

"Want supper," he said when Jack Munson brought a glass of whiskey.

"Take a table. Cindy will get to you." Munson was an old school barman. Always dressed in a fine linen shirt with a full-length white apron. He took pride in his bar and was offended when Jimmy the Cueball intimated that he served his liquor in dirty glassware.

Jimmy looked about and spotted little Cindy Payton serving supper at tables in the back, grabbed his bottle and headed that way. *You're damn right she'll get to me, and she better make it quick. Wonder how much she costs? Too much, whatever it is.*

"Howdy, stranger. What can I get you?" Cindy Payton had a smile for everyone, made her little restaurant an area of friendly chatter and good food, but wished she hadn't smiled this time. She felt an immediate fear; his blazing, squinty eyes undressed her, there was danger in those thin lips that wouldn't smile, and the numerous scars on his face spoke of a mean and vicious person.

"I said I want supper. Don't be gettin' all high-falutin' on me. Whatcha got for me, sweetie?"

She wanted to run, but instead, said. "Got beef steaks, elk roast, and lamb chops on the menu tonight." She stood back as far from him as she could and thought she could run if he tried something.

"Gimme a steak, and don't burn it to death. You available for the night?" Get right to the point, Jimmy always said. "Need a room, too."

She recoiled at the comment, backing up another step. "Not me, Buster, don't do those things. Rooms are all booked, too. One steak dinner coming up," she said and turned to head back to the kitchen.

Jimmy the Cueball jumped up and grabbed the girl, spun her around and slapped her hard across the side of her head, sending her across the room and into a table where Ed Lindstrom and Amos White were having supper. White kept little Cindy from crashing to the floor and eased her into a chair.

"Better explain yourself, mister," Amos White said, stepping across to where Jimmy stood.

"Woman's got a bitter mouth," Jimmy said. "I just set her straight. Don't you be getting in my face just cuz you're wearin' a badge? She gave me the smart mouth and I gave it back. Needs to learn her place."

"Seems more likely that you do, mister. Turn around and put your hands up, nice and slow." Amos White was at least twice as big as Jimmy the Cueball and he took another step toward the outlaw.

"I will not," Jimmy said, softly. He was incredibly

fast, pulling his Colt, but found himself flung backward, crashing into a table behind him, bleeding from a wound high on his shoulder. The pistol was flung from his grasp from the force of the bullet smashing bone and muscle. There was a cry of pain as he crashed onto the floor. He'd never been bested before and sat on the floor with a dumb look on his face.

"I'm a better shot than that," Amos White said, turning to Ed Lindstrom. "Meant to kill him."

"Corcoran's gonna love you, Mister White." A crowd was gathering around, getting too close to the wounded man. "It's all over folks. Step back now and give us room to do our job."

Amos White got the bleeding man to his feet and slapped him hard, the open-handed hit could be heard out on the street, sending Jimmy back to the floor. "Men don't hit women if I'm around, mister. It don't matter none whether I'm wearin' a badge. Get up."

Lindstrom was helping get Cindy Payton into the kitchen to get her face washed in cold water. "Come on, girl, let's get you cleaned up. You'll be fine, honey." Two of the saloon girls rushed over and took her from the deputy, and he turned his attention to White and the prisoner. "We'll take him to Doc Weatherford's first, Amos. That was some shooting."

"Yeah, well, fast is good but accurate is better, is

what my pa always said. I wasn't accurate."

Ed Lindstrom thought that with that kind of shooting, his idea of accurate was the difference between a high shoulder hit and a heart hit. *I wish I was that kind of inaccurate.* He was still chuckling as they hustled Jimmy the Cueball out of the saloon. "Take him to Doc's and I'll find Corcoran."

"All right, Buster, let's move," Amos said. "You got a name?" No answer and Jimmy tried to twist away from the big deputy, crying out in pain from the wound. "We'll just stick with Buster for the time being. Stupid comes to mind," Lindstrom chuckled. "Maybe Ass." He shoved him hard getting another cry of pain.

"You just go ahead and cry it out, Buster. Men that hit women need to know that there are consequences. Does this hurt?" He put strong fingers around the man's shoulder and heard the gasp and howl of pain. "Yup, that hurt. Good. Sure wish I'd been a better shot, though."

"Wouldn't have to listen to this little boy if you had been," Lindstrom chuckled.

CHAPTER FIVE

"This is exactly what I told Dupree would happen if he let Jimmy come into town by himself," Oscar Owens muttered, standing at the end of the bar, sipping brandy. "That damn kid will be the end of this job." He had to get out to that cabin and let Dupree know what just happened. "Kinkaid is sure to hear. Hope he's smart enough to come to the cabin."

The storm rolled in as expected with cold temperatures, winds picking up and gusting, and people getting home as quickly as possible. Big, soft flakes of snow were starting to swirl in the winds as the first storm of the season moved into the Diamond Range. Owens cussed for the entire ride to the cabin and found Dupree eating supper in a toasty room. "Cueball's in jail, shot by a deputy. Why'd you let him come to town alone, Clarence? First thing he did was whack some woman in a restaurant. He's plumb crazy, you know."

"I know but I got tired of hearing the whining and told him to go. He's worse than a little girl when he gets to whining. Think he'll give us away?"

"Think? Hell, man, he's a weasel. First chance he gets. A little offer of easy time and he'll spit our plans all over that jail. He talks big about that so-called Mexican jail, but he's a weakling, Dupree, and the one of us that shouldn't have been caught. Hope Kinkaid hears about it and heads out here. We need to make some drastic changes to our plans." Owens wanted to tell Dupree just how stupid it was for him to let Jimmy ride off alone, but held back.

"It was Kinkaid in the Mexican jail. Never mind. What we need to do is ride to town and kill Cueball. That bald head of his can't much talk if it's dead."

"Yeah, but we wouldn't be in this position if you'd kept him with you. I stood right there at the end of the bar and watched the whole thing. That deputy pulled faster than anything I've ever seen."

Dupree poured a glass of whiskey and laughed right out. "Shove a Colt up his nose and pull the trigger, Oscar, that's what I need to do. Let's ride, find Joey, kill Cueball, and head west."

"West?"

"Sure as hell we can't stay here and rob trains and

banks, now can we? Reno's filled with money. Cueball's got a dumb head, stupid, and will tell them everything we've planned."

"Not if we kill him tonight." Owens was tired of running. From Dodge City to Cheyenne, to Salt Lake, and now to Eureka, they hadn't stopped for more than a week in any one place. Case a bank, hit it, and run, over and over. "I'd really like to follow through on this one, Dupree. There's enough money on those trains that we wouldn't ever have to run again. I want to sit in a hammock, bottle at hand, serenaded by some señorita."

The dream had been there from the day he turned forty years old. *Running. Always running from something, from someone. Just sit under a tree, or on a patio, with warm sunshine, cool water, good liquor, and fine women.* Oscar Owens had pulled his first job as a young boy, worked with an uncle stealing horses in one county and selling them two counties away, then running into the hills until things cooled off. "I'm tired of running, Dupree. One nice fat coach full of gold and silver coins, and my last run to Mexico."

"Let's find Joey, take care of Jimmy the Cueball, and then we'll talk about it. A stranger making a ruckus is sure to bring questions. All the talk I've heard about this Corcoran feller, though, worries me."

"I don't know about Corcoran but the one I saw tonight would test both of us."

They rode back to town through heavy snowfall, the temperature was nearing the zero mark when they came into the sleeping little village. The only lights were at the Bonanza Club and a few scattered cabins. "Know where Joey's staying?" Dupree asked.

"Said he had a camp outside of town. Doesn't like buildings, he said. With this storm he might just be at the saloon," he chuckled. "Walls or not."

A few men were playing cards, more lined up at the bar, and Clarence Dupree and Oscar Owens had plenty of room at the bar. A roaring fire in the large, potbelly stove along with the many bodies warmed the place nicely. They ordered whiskey and watched Joey Kinkaid and Henry Carter walk out of the back corner of the restaurant. He spotted them and came right over.

"Storm drive you in, did it? Sure did me. This here's Henry Carter. Works part-time as a deputy. He just told me that some guy tried to get tough with one of the girls in here and got shot by the deputies."

Dupree had to smile that Kinkaid didn't mention anything about Jimmy the Cueball being a friend of his. Owens nodded his thanks. "Some men ain't too smart. Men like that need to die," Owens muttered, and Joey Kinkaid got the message.

"Yeah, they do," Kinkaid said. "What did you say they did with that fool?" He asked Carter.

"Old Doc Weatherford was worried about heavy bleeding and said he wanted to keep him at his place overnight instead of putting him in a cell. Corcoran argued but the doc's pretty demanding sometimes. He's got both legs chained to the bed and the doc kicked everyone out."

"Nobody guarding a mean sumbitch like that? Man that would beat on a woman?" Dupree seemed almost angry about that. "We should do something about that. You're a deputy, let's make sure that desperado ain't gonna get away."

"No, Doc wouldn't like that. No, I think Corcoran's right around close anyway. I gotta go. Joey, gentlemen," and Henry Carter headed for home through the deepening snow. Naive is too weak a word to describe Carter's actions.

"Sounded like he gave us an open invitation to visit that wounded outlaw," Kinkaid joshed.

"So the sheriff is watching from the outside. How do we get past him? Maybe a little ruckus?" Dupree had a slight grin on his face. "Gotta get that man dead before they have a chance to talk to him."

"A little ruckus might not bring the sheriff but a couple of gunshots sure as hell will." Oscar Owens signaled for some more whiskey. "You still up on your trick shots, Dupree. It's worked before."

"Ain't practiced in some time but it's more timing than anything. Hell yes, a couple of gunshots has always brought the sheriff," he laughed.

"You know where the doc's place is, Joey?" Kinkaid nodded. "Good. Let's you and me get over near there, and in fifteen minutes or so, Dupree, you put on some kind of shooting demonstration to draw that big old mean sheriff away.

"One like you pulled in Denver would work well." They all laughed remembering how Dupree had shot out candles in the chandeliers enabling the men to steal money from the gambling tables. Everyone amazed that he could snuff out the candles without breaking them, and then it was dark. "We'll go in and kill Jimmy the Cueball just as easy as we took all the table's money."

They toasted the plan, and Kinkaid and Owens slipped out of the saloon and walked up the main street in snow already inches deep. "See the house with the lights and heavy smoke coming out the chimney? That's the doc's place," Kinkaid said.

"Let's just get in those trees and watch for a few minutes," Owens said.

It wasn't long and they spotted Corcoran near one

of the lit windows, hunkered down near a rain barrel. "We better get around over that way, Joey," Owens said. "When Dupree starts shooting out the lights or throwing coins and shooting them, that sheriff will come running right at us." He tried to hold in his chuckle but couldn't. "That would ruin our plans, eh?"

They backtracked some, worked around a building and came up on the other side of where Corcoran was hidden. Within moments, two quick shots were heard, then two more. Corcoran jumped to his feet and, when two more shots were fired, ran hard for the saloon.

"Let's go," Owens said, racing for the front door of the house, smashing their way through and back toward the room that was lit. That door splintered when Joey Kinkaid hit it at a full run and they found Doc Weatherford standing over Jimmy the Cueball. Owens pushed the doc aside and Kinkaid ran up to the wounded man.

"Glad you're here, men. Free me up," Jimmy said.

"We're here to set you free," Kinkaid said, and put two rounds through Jimmy's head.

"Run," Owens said as they backtracked through the house and out onto the snow-covered street. They raced as hard as they could to their horses and rode fast out of town. The snow was falling hard, driven by icy winds that swirled it into drifts that were getting deep. They rode out of the canyon, down into the Diamond Valley, and after about ten minutes slowed down to a walk.

"We need to split up, Kinkaid. Dupree will be expecting us at the cabin tomorrow sometime, but we don't want to lead a posse in either. You got some place to go?"

"Can't get to my camp. It's on the other side of town. I'll ride in circles out through the sagebrush. That usually throws a posse off, then tuck in under an outcrop of rock 'till sunrise."

"Good. Hope it keeps snowing and covers these tracks. See you tomorrow," Oscar Owens said. He put his horse in a fast trot right up the main road north through the valley.

Dupree sipped his whiskey for at least fifteen minutes after the boys left, then slammed his bottle hard on the bar top. "Any of you boys really good with a gun? I mean really good?" He flipped a silver dollar into the aid, drew his Colt, and shot twice, hitting it once.

"Well, just damn me," he said. "Missed." He flipped another cartwheel up and fired twice more, hitting it both times. "That's better. Think I can do that again?" He laughed at the bartender, and Jack Munson threw two cartwheels in the air. Dupree shot twice, hitting both. "By damn, that was fun," he said, shucking empty shells on the bar and reloading.

"Anyone else want to try?"

The gunfire brought Jimmy Henderson racing down the stairs from his office. "What the hell's going on?" He demanded. "What's all the shooting?"

Munson started to explain when Corcoran came rushing through the doors, gun in hand. "What's going on?" He said, looking about for what the problem might be. That's when he heard two shots from some distance. "Damn," he howled, spinning around and racing out the doors in time to hear two horses galloping off.

He ran as hard as his long legs would go to Doc's, saw the busted doors and found Doc Weatherford standing over Jimmy the Cueball's body. "Nicely done," he murmured, and walked out into the snowstorm.

Dupree bowed to Jimmy Henderson, said something about good shooting, and walked out to his horse. He rode out of town, crisscrossing the trail left by Kinkaid and Owens. A walking horse would often drag his front feet, and Dupree did a good job of partially obliterating their trail.

Corcoran and Sandy McAuliff were sitting with Henderson at a table, Betty Cord standing next to Corcoran. "That was well executed, Jimmy. They drew me away from the wounded man as if I was a damn mouse chasing cheese. Amos White and I are gonna see if we can find their trail, but it snowed all night."

It was late, but Corcoran found himself looking around for Cindy Payton. "Is Cindy going to be okay. Did that fool hurt her bad?"

"No, not serious bad," Betty said. "She'll be bruised and sore for a week, though."

Corcoran was more than despondent, swirled his coffee around and drummed his long fingers on the table. "I haven't been set up like that in a long time. I showed the posters to Weatherford and he said the one that shot our outlaw was Joey Kinkaid. The man shooting in here has to have been Clarence Dupree, and the other was Oscar Owens. Don't know who the dead man is."

"This was the gang that Peter Bridges was sure about?" Henderson stood up and walked around the table. It was starting to get light outside but still snowing. The wind blew all night, heavy snow fell, and the likelihood of following the outlaws' trail was slim. "Think they'll hang around?"

"With this storm? If they didn't ride north to Palisade and grab a fast freight, they're still close by," Corcoran said. "I'm gonna squash 'em, shoot 'em dead, and hang 'em, too. Damn, did they get one on me? Ed

Connor won't like the way I'm running his office. I better get with Lindstrom and White.

"Sandy, you're now a Eureka County deputy again. Take care of the office, will you?" McAuliff nodded, knowing just how deep the hurt was for Corcoran. He wanted to say something and knew anything he said wouldn't be taken well.

"I'll keep that jail clean and warm, Irish. Go find those fools." *God help anybody who crosses him today. Trouble with people like Corcoran is, they feel they have to be perfect all the time, and at my age, I know there just ain't nobody that's perfect.*

Just as he figured, Corcoran and Lindstrom found no tracks leading out of town. No one was moving and the snow was deep. "They rode out this way, Ed, but there are hundreds of places to hide out there. If you were a crook, where would you hide?"

"If I was planning to rob the bank and needed someplace to make those plans? It would be close, Terrence. Within five miles, and hidden from view. Off any main road or trail."

"Yeah, me too. Up in the mountains, deep in a canyon, surrounded by trees and outcrops. Bring anything to mind?"

Lindstrom was laughing as they turned back toward town. "Sounds like a perfect place to build a line shack or hunting cabin to me. Of course, there are line shacks all over. Every rancher summers his herd high in the mountains. They aren't used in the winter, so anyone could sit out a few weeks and nobody would know it. They all have food, cots, and a good wood stove."

They rode back to the office and found it just as warm as Sandy McAuliff promised it would be. "No tracks, eh?"

Corcoran scowled but nodded, pouring some fresh coffee. He described what he and Lindstrom had discussed as a hiding place. "You're one of the best trackers in this area, Sandy. Bring anything to mind?"

"Only about a dozen or so," he chuckled. "There are line camps all over these mountains, Terrence. Did those boys ride north into Diamond Valley or head west?"

"No tracks out there to tell, Sandy." Corcoran paced around the office, poured more coffee, and finally sat down. "These men have been in town for several days, apparently, and that means they have had conversations with some of our residents. I'm going over to the Bonanza and see if Jack at the bar or Jimmy have noticed."

Bundled again in his buffalo robe coat and beat up

old sombrero pulled down tight, he stepped back onto the street. *They gotta be close, and with this cold, they gotta be inside something. Sandy said that Colonel Cornell had talked with one of them, but he's a serious nut case. I wonder who else they have talked with?*

"Mornin' Jack," Corcoran said to barman Jack Munson at the Bonanza Club. "You were here when that fool put on his little shooting demonstration last night?"

"You bet, Terrence. Good shootin', too."

"Yeah," Corcoran growled. "Well-timed. Has he been in a lot? The shooter?"

"Only seen him a few times. New around here. That feller with him has a room here. Don't remember hearing any names, though."

Corcoran was glad to hear that the man he thought was Oscar Owens had a room at the hotel. "Did either of them have any local friends, or did they talk with anyone?"

"The heavy one, the shooter, didn't talk much to anyone. Just growled out what he wanted, but the younger one seemed to have regular conversations with old Henry Carter. Henry'd close his store and come in for a drink and the two would talk for some time."

Corcoran had to chuckle. *All my life as a lawman and it never fails. If you want to know anything about a village, go to the saloon and ask the barman. They know everything about everyone.* "Henry Carter, eh? That's interesting." He had a million questions but knew better than to ask them. Was Carter in on the gang's plans? Was he helping the gang? Was that why he's been pressing so hard to be a full-time deputy? *I'll have to find those answers myself.*

He was interrupted by Colonel Buford S. Cornell, blustering his way up to the bar. "Hear tell you lost a prisoner last night, Corcoran. Ain't the way we did things in the big war. No, sir, not the way we held those Johnny Rebs. No escapin' neither."

"You got a bad mouth, Colonel, or is it, Mister Cornell? I have heard tall tales of you hanging around with this man Dupree. Want to tell me about that?" Corcoran was ready to fire every bullet he carried into the fool, but fought it off.

"Nothin' to tell. The man's looking to open a bank around these parts and needed some expert advice. That's what I do, Corcoran. I'm an expert at my work."

"So's Dupree, Cornell. He's a wanted man, wanted for bank robbing and killing. That makes you a known associate, Mr. Expert." Cornell jumped back at that comment, tried to say something and Corcoran just shook him off. He pointed at the front door and Cornell got the message immediately. Corcoran had to chuckle but still wanted to shoot the man.

"Is Jimmy upstairs?" Corcoran spotted Betty Cord walking across the large saloon toward him. Jack Munson nodded yes, but Corcoran waited for Betty instead.

"Morning Sheriff. Acting, that is," she smiled. He tipped his hat and smiled back at the lovely lady. She was wearing a full-length gown, so he wanted another glimpse of those long legs.

"A ray of sunshine has arrived," he said. "Did you ever talk to the man who did the shooting in here last night? Or his companion?"

"Both men always drank at the bar, never gambled either," she said. "He sure was a fine shooter, though."

"He's a wanted bank robber and gunman, Betty. That shooting was to draw me in here so his friends could kill my prisoner, the man that whipped on Cindy. I know you've only been here a short time, but have you heard anything about any of those men in here last night?"

"The older of the men has a room here and the young one is friends with one of your deputies. The man that has a store. Carter, I think is his name. The heavy man, the shooter, has been in but isn't very friendly."

Two people have said the same thing about Henry Carter, Corcoran was thinking. *Maybe it's time I paid our part-time deputy a little visit. He's not that kind of man. Taking care of a sick mother, raising two children without benefit of a wife, and owning a store too? Henry's being used and doesn't know it. Strangers come to town looking for information about banks and railroads and a part-time deputy is too naive to recognize what they're doing? Glad I found Amos White.*

CHAPTER SIX

"Hello the cabin." Oscar Owens yelled out well before riding in close. "Don't shoot."

"Ride on in. Let me see you." Dupree yelled back.

Owens rode up to the hitch rack and stepped down. "Hope you got a good fire going."

"Have any trouble riding in? Anyone try to follow?" Clarence Dupree was sitting at the table in the little shack, holding his rifle in one hand and a coffee cup in the other, when Oscar Owens walked in. He had the fire going all night, hoping that his two remaining gang members would make it back. He had ridden straight to the cabin, assuming that his tracks would be covered by sunrise. Wind was a friend to those not wishing to leave a trace.

Owens had ridden all night through deepening drifts of blowing snow, making every effort to give the appearance of a lost rider. He was covered in ice and was fighting to get out of his heavy winter coat. "Haven't seen a living thing," he grinned. It took an effort to get out of his iced Mackinaw and he flung it over a chair and stood next to the stove. "Heard from Joey?"

"Expected you'd be riding together. Smart though, separating like that," Dupree said. "They'll go through your hotel room, you know. Leave anything there that can come back on us?"

"Some dirty clothes is all," Owens grinned. He tightened up some hearing a horse stomp its feet just outside the door. "Hope that's Joey." Both he and Dupree had their guns out and cocked when Joey Kinkaid came through the door. "Need to yell out next time, Kinkaid. Could'a shot you dead."

"Cold," Kinkaid said getting as close to the stove as he could. "Bullet wouldn't go through this much ice," he chuckled. "Whiskey," he said when Owens offered him some coffee. "Just whiskey until I know I'm alive. Must be a hundred below out there. Never saw another person, though."

"There's just the three of us now and a little town with a rich bank." Dupree poured whiskey in his coffee and looked at the two men. "The town now knows we are all together and it won't take much thought to know why."

"Best bet, Dupree, is for us to head west and hit little towns on our way to Reno and then Virginia City. Lots of money there." Kinkaid had talked about the Comstock riches all the way from Dodge City.

Oscar Owens was tired of running but knew their chances of getting anything out of Eureka were zero. "All three of us were standing together at the bar just before Cueball met his end. They'll be watching for sure."

"Still, that's no reason to leave empty handed, Oscar. All we need to know before we leave is the train schedules and that kid at the bank, Johnny Lewis, was getting those for us. Can you get in to see him?"

"Damn," Owens said. He was pacing around the table, getting close to the stove, then pacing some more. "That kid wants to ride with us, too, Dupree. We need a fourth person. Let's wait a day or two and I'll ride in and find him. Problem is everyone in town knows me and that kid don't know either one of you. Gonna get me hung, Dupree." He poured more whiskey than coffee and looked around the stark cabin.

"If we were still talking about the bank, I'd want to back out, but if we're talking about taking out the train, I'm with it. I am worrying about getting in and out of town to talk to that jerk kid."

"You'll do fine," Dupree said. Owens saw the little

smile and wanted to shoot the man dead. "If they think we're gonna hit that bank, they'll really be surprised when we hit the train instead. Don't let that kid know our real target. Make sure he thinks it's the bank we want."

"Show me Oscar Owens' room, Betty," Corcoran said. "Jack, if Jimmy Henderson comes down, tell him where I am." They went upstairs and back into the hotel part of the building. "He get any visitors?"

"That man with the white hair and beard, the one who calls himself Colonel Something. He's been up a couple of times, and some kid, Johnny Something. He's never had one of the working girls up, though," she smiled.

"Did this Johnny kid wear a nice looking business suit and carry a sidearm?" Corcoran was starting to see a pattern and didn't like what he was seeing. The colonel was a blow-hard, but could take in those willing to be taken in. He told anyone listening that he knew banking inside and out. And if this kid was Johnny Lewis, then the gang's aim was, sure as hell, the bank.

Old man Bridges had taken in the Lewis kid when he was about fourteen. The Lewis couple were killed in a bad fire and Bridges took in the kid, teaching him the banking business. Johnny Lewis was a smart-Alex from the day he was born, bragged about taking over the bank when Bridges kicked off, and swaggered in new, store-bought clothing. Many thought Bridges was wrong, that Lewis was no good, would have grown to be an outlaw, sure as all.

She gave Corcoran a curious look and said, "Why, yes. Do you know him?"

"I'm afraid so," he said.

He spent just a few minutes going through the small hotel room, finding only dirty trail wear. No notes, no detailed drawings of Peter Bridges' bank, and no lists of names. Jimmy Henderson stuck his head in the doorway. "Find anything?"

"Nope, not here, but Betty Cord gave me a good little tip. Johnny Lewis come around here often?"

"That arrogant little snot's been hanging around with this man," Henderson said. "Ever since Bridges took him in and gave him a job, he's got his nose stuck high enough to scrape the ceiling, Corcoran."

"Thanks," Corcoran said. He gave Betty Cord a hug, kissed the top of her head, and took the stairs two at a time as he headed for the bank and a talk with Bridges. *So all of Bridges' worries about his bank being hit might not just be worries. Henderson's place could very well be next. Who else have these people used for information?* It was a half block walk up to the bank through heavy snow, and he had a question going through his mind for each step he took.

"Johnny Lewis?" Peter Bridges sat in his big wing back chair, fully astonished that young Lewis might be working with the potential bank robbers. "Are you sure, Corcoran? My God, Johnny?" He pulled a flask from a bottom drawer and took a long swallow. "I'll call him in and give him a bloody thrashing."

"No, Peter, don't. Not yet." Corcoran took the offered flask for a belt himself. "What information would he have to give? The combinations? The schedules of shipments in and out? When the bank would be completely empty?"

Peter Bridges sat back in his chair with an almost defeated look on his face. "I trusted that boy as if he were my son," he said, quietly. "Except for the combinations, he would know all of that." Corcoran could see the anger building in the big man. "That little bastard," he said.

"Let's not give away our secret, here, Bridges. That gang might very well be hiding in a nearby line shack, still planning on taking this bank. Lewis doesn't know we're on to him. What would be happening soon that would excite these men?"

"We have a large shipment of coin and cash coming in from San Francisco next week, Corcoran. I haven't even put out the notice yet."

"Good," Corcoran said. "That would excite any bank robber." Both men were chuckling softly, but Bridges was the softest. "How does that work, putting out the notice?"

"I simply post it at the cage. Which day, which train, since sometimes more than one train a day arrives, and what the shipment contains. The shipment will be transferred to a wagon and brought to the bank, using my own guards. This is a fairly regular occurrence, Corcoran."

"And Lewis would know all of that?" He got a nod back from the banker and sat still for a moment. In his mind, the time to hit would be at the transfer from the train to the wagon. *It feels like I'm back in Virginia City. That's the way they tried it there. We'll make these fellers into fools this time.*

"He would know the exact time of the train's arrival?" Again, Bridges nodded. Corcoran knew that there was at least one and often more, trains daily into Eureka. "What day is that shipment arriving, Peter?" *I'm gonna trap me a load of bank robbers and send half of them to hell. In particular the one that pulled a fast one on me.*

Oscar Owens was riding slow and carefully toward Eureka early in the morning. "How the hell am I gonna find this kid without being seen?" He had a canvas duster over his Mackinaw, his hat was pulled down tight, and he kept his head tucked low. Johnny Lewis had told Owens where he lived and it took several minutes for the man to find the place. "That damn kid lives with the banker? This isn't good," he said. He tied off his horse and crept up to the kitchen door.

Lewis opened the door to Owens' soft knocking and they got inside without being seen. "Whole town's looking for you," the kid said. "Sherif's been to the bank a couple of times."

"Fix up a pot of coffee Johnny, and we'll have a nice little talk about that. You never said you lived with the banker. You settin' us up, cuz if I find out you are, I'll rip your guts and spread them for the magpies."

"No, no," Lewis said. "The old fool took me in when my folks was killed. I hate that guy and want to be a part of what you are doing. I want what that old man has."

Owens wasn't sure whether to believe him or not, but needed the railroad schedule. "We're gonna need your information to make this work, and you'll get a full share for your efforts. You all the way in? Don't lie to me."

The kid's eyes were wide and the smile wider when he heard full share. "Yeah, sure," he said. He was cocky enough as a clerk in training at Bridges' bank, but to be in the gang for a full share for robbing that bank? He wanted to shout it out. "I ain't lying. What is it you need?"

Oscar Owens spent the morning with Lewis going over the best way in and out of the bank, where the most money would be found, and Owens finally got to what he really wanted. "We need to know when the bank holds the largest amount of money," he said.

"That would be when a shipment arrives for the mines and for us. The schedules were just posted yesterday. The mine shipment is scheduled for next Tuesday morning."

Owens wanted a whole lot more than that, and pressed for the exact time of arrival. "We want to hit that bank when that shipment is being hauled into the building, Johnny, so times are very important. What time does the train arrive in Eureka?"

"He gave you the exact time?" Dupree found that amazing. "How would that kid know that?"

"He said Peter Bridges posts the times so all the clerks know it. Everybody at that bank is armed all the time. What's our plan now?"

Dupree got out a map showing the rail line down the valley. There were water stops that ranchers used to board the trains, but one seemed the best. "Palisade is where the narrow gauge meets the main line, then going south there are water stops at Raines, Blackburn, Alpha, and Garden Pass. See here, at Garden Pass? It's high, the train has to slow way down getting across that pass. That's where we hit it. We'll have that money, ride like the wind back toward the main east-west road, and be on our way to Reno."

Dupree sat back in his chair with a big smile. "The kid thinks we're gonna hit the bank?"

"Yup," Owens smiled. "I told him we'd give him a full share of the loot and he'd be a member of our gang." Even hard-nosed Joey Kinkaid had to laugh along with the others.

"That gives us three days to get ready," Dupree said. "After we stop the train, we gotta remember to cut the wires. What's the best way to stop the train?"

"That's part of why you got the dynamite, Dupree. We blow the rails with some of it, and blow the money coach with the rest. It will take almost a day to get to Garden Pass because of this snow, so let's make sure we're packed right and have enough food to get north after the hit. This isn't the time to get sloppy.

"Kinkaid, you said you've worked with dynamite before, and I know you have, Dupree, but just so we remember that we want to come out of this alive, pack the blasting caps and fuse on one horse and the dynamite on another. Never on the same horse. Just in case," he said with a slight chuckle.

CHAPTER SEVEN

Corcoran was at the sheriff's desk pouring some brandy in his tin coffee cup. Ed Lindstrom, Sandy McAuliff, Henry Carter, and Amos White were scattered around the desk but close to that potbelly stove. The cold had settled in following the big snowstorm, with wind whipping through the canyon. Corcoran had insisted that Carter be at the meeting despite all the arguments against it by Lindstrom.

"He's been telling that gang all about this department right along, Terrence. He needs to be horsewhipped not invited in." Corcoran agreed with Lindstrom but insisted.

"There's nothing worse than a lawman gone bad, Ed. But I want Carter there. You'll understand." Corcoran could be devious, those men working with him fully understood, but to bring Carter in as if he was a regular member of the department? Even Sandy McAuliff wanted to argue the point.

"We had ways of gettin' even with them kinds of people back when I was scoutin' for the army. Hang 'em high and tell 'em bye," he laughed along with everyone else, including Corcoran.

"I'm glad we're all here because it's about to get very active around these parts. A shipment of cash and coins is arriving in three days and this little gang we've been seeing around town is about to hit. So are we. There will be one more person coming in, and I'll wait for her before going into details."

Her? Everyone looked around, looked at each other, and no one had an answer. Why would Corcoran be bringing a woman to the meeting? First, he invites Carter? Now, a woman? Nobody said a word, though.

Coffee and alcoholic additives were spread around before Betty Cord came into the small office. "Morning, boys," she chirped. "Cold out there." Her smile added about eight degrees to the temperature, based on the color in the boys' faces. Corcoran helped her out of a heavy wool coat and she got close to the stove. "You told me why I was supposed to be here, Terrence, but you're not going to make me wear a badge, are you?"

"No, I'm not," Corcoran chuckled. "but we have a

problem about to come to the surface and we do need your help in keeping it under control. Besides the obvious, anything you might hear this morning is just between all of us, not the rest of the town." He chuckled again, looked around the room and Betty could see a cold dark cloud come across his face. He stood up from the desk and strode around to stand in front of Henry Carter.

"Henry, we have a problem that needs correcting before we can lay out our plans. You've been meeting with this man, Joey Kinkaid, on a regular basis, and Kinkaid is wanted for murder and bank robbery in half a dozen areas. I don't know why, don't want to hear any of your reasons. I'm putting you under arrest right now for your associating with wanted criminals."

Carter jumped to his feet and started to say something. Corcoran pushed him back down, hard. "Your business will remain until a judge figures out what to do with you. I've asked Betty Cord to handle your business affairs and to spend time looking after your mother and your children. Sandy, would you take the man into custody and place him in one of your cells, please?"

Carter made a dash for the door only to get smashed over the head with the heavy end of a Colt revolver. "No, no, Mr. Carter," Ed Lindstrom said. "Now I know why you wanted him here, Corcoran. Good play." He and Sandy McAuliff jerked Henry Carter to his wobbly and uncertain feet and hustled him into one of the cells in the back part of the building.

"Get his keys so Betty has access to his store and the house," Corcoran yelled. He turned to Betty and gave her a big smile. "You're a gem for doing this. His kids are young, his mother is old and bed-ridden, and this is a big job you're taking on."

"I know," she said. "but why didn't you just come out and ask me about this?" She was smiling but confused by Corcoran's actions. "I hope you don't think that just because I like you, you can get me to do things like this. This is a huge responsibility."

"It is indeed and you're the only person I know who could do this. You're single, responsible, and the kind of person who can help. It's a part of your soul, Betty, and your eyes."

"His family isn't a part of Mr. Carter's problem and they need taking care of. You knew, didn't you, that I'd take care of those kids and the old lady? It's just the way I am," she said. "Obvious, eh?"

"I'm glad you're the way you are." He gave a little grin followed by a wink, and she almost giggled. "Carter's son is six now, and the little girl is only three," Corcoran said. "Their mother was killed when a buggy crashed into the creek south of town. It's a big responsibility."

"With children, his mother, the store, why would Carter turn outlaw? It doesn't make much sense to me," she said. "I was in his little store and it was busy. He's not hurting for money, can get help for the kids and his mother, so what's behind this?"

"Maybe, just maybe, we'll get to find out, but I doubt it. I've never understood the mind of an outlaw." He shook his head, poured coffee for the two of them, laced his with some brandy, and slipped an arm around her waist. "There is a possibility that he is simply naive, didn't even recognize the problem." He could see in her eyes that she hoped that was the answer. "If you need anything, come to me, Betty, and we'll try to get what you need. Well, I mean, oh, hell. Just come to me and smile and you can have the world," he said.

She wrapped her arms around the big man and gave him a long kiss, getting loud cheers from Sandy McAuliff, coming back into the room, and Ed Lindstrom. "Knock it off," Corcoran tried to snarl, but it didn't work.

Lindstrom handed a set of keys to Betty and she left to start her next project. "Now, let's talk about tomorrow." Corcoran got everyone settled, fresh coffee served, and cigars lit. "My God, I'm even starting to sound like Ed Connor," he laughed.

"You're ugly enough," Sandy McAuliff chortled. "And, gettin' long in the tooth."

Corcoran humphed a bit, hid a grim, and tried to ignore the comment. "That train is due at the station at 10:07 Tuesday morning and I believe that's when the Owens' gang is going to hit. What Owens doesn't know is this. There won't be a dime on that train. The schedule was altered by a day and all that money arrived this morning. It is safely tucked away in Bridges' vault right now."

"You are a cagey devil, Corcoran. How'd you pull that off?" Lindstrom had to chuckle thinking how the bandits would react to an empty money coach.

"It was scheduled for today right along. All Peter did was alter the schedule he posted for his employees. It's Johnny Lewis who got the big surprise when that shipment came in. I was standing next to him and laid my hand on his shoulder when the wagon pulled up. He and Carter will have something to talk about back there, at least."

"I thought I recognized him," Ed Lindstrom said. "You don't have any paperwork filed on his arrest."

"Nope. Henry Carter might have seen it," Corcoran said. This time the grin was spread fully across the craggy old face. "That boy about soiled his pants."

After considerable laughter and loud talk, it was time to get down to business. "It will take all of us to take these fools down. Bridges will have his regular complement of guards at the station when the train pulls in. We need to be spread around the area, but as much out of sight as possible. We're gonna need your sharp-shooting abilities, Mr. Lindstrom. If you have any questions, don't wait until tomorrow, if not, let's get outside and be seen around town. No talk with anyone about tomorrow."

"If you're talking sharp-shooting, you better include Amos White. Damn fool was upset because he was off by an inch when he shot that fool that whupped on little Cindy Payton."

Ed Lindstrom and Sandy McAuliff were near the cattle loading chutes while Corcoran and Amos White were standing just inside the large sliding doors of the rail-side warehouse. "Something's wrong," Corcoran said, checking his watch again. "Only foul weather keeps these trains off schedule. Train's almost ten minutes late. Come on, White," he said and loped toward the office and ticket window.

"Any word?" He hollered at the telegraph operator.

"No, but I'm sure there's a problem. I just sent a wire to Palisade and they haven't answered. Line's down, somewhere."

"They hit the train before it got here," Corcoran growled. "Come on," he said again to Amos White. Corcoran ran to Sandy McAuliff. "We're riding again, Mr. McAuliff. Go home and pack your saddlebags for two days. No mules on this ride. Amos White, do the same thing. The two of you meet me in front of the Bonanza Club muy pronto. Ed, the town is yours. Keep it safe."

Corcoran rode fast to the Bonanza and found Cindy Payton in the kitchen. "I need three pounds of smoked meat and a sack of beans, darlin'. Better throw in a pound of coffee beans, too. How you feelin'?"

"I'm just sore, Terrence," she said. All of the natural ebullience of the lady was gone. She didn't leap into his arms, throw herself at him with hugs and kisses. Just stood there, dull eyes looking more at the floor than him. "Bruised up like a barroom hussy," she chuckled.

She put his stuff together quickly, got a hug and kiss, and Corcoran was out the door. He stopped at the bar and talked Jack Munson out of a bottle of brandy for the ride, and was in front of the sheriff's office minutes later.

"We'll follow the rail tracks out, gentlemen, but what we find might not be pretty. Those boys are gonna be angry outlaws when they find out there's no money on that train." The morning was cold and clear with just a gentle breeze blowing. Wrapped in their winter finery, the posse rode at a fast trot out of town.

The first several miles were through rolling ground on the main road north, which ran alongside the tracks. When they moved into rougher country they had to slow down some, fighting heavy snow in the shady places and mud in others. The wind hadn't let up at all and despite the bright sun, it was bitter cold.

Garden Pass was at the southern end of the Sulphur Springs Range and was at about six thousand feet. The watering station sat at the top of a long climb, and the trains were at their slowest if passing through. Corcoran saw the smoke long before they reached the wreck. Instead of simply blowing the rails to stop the train, it looked like they had laid in the dynamite to go off as the engine passed over. The blast ruptured the working parts of the locomotive creating a massive blast that killed the engineer and fireman.

Three of the five cars had jumped the rails and overturned, and the other two sat cockeyed, half on and half off the rails. The only person alive was the conductor, Jimmy Baines, who had been riding in the caboose. There was no armored coach. "This was a freight run," Conductor Baines said. "Thank God there were no passenger cars." He wiped blood from his face.

"Those men were so angry they torched the cars, Sheriff. They even took the pocket watch from the dead engineer." Baines had cuts and bruises but no broken bones or gunshot wounds. Corcoran had Baines ride behind Amos White back to Eureka.

"Have Lindstrom put together a work crew to fix the telegraph wires and bring these bodies in. Word of this needs to get out," Corcoran told White. "When you finish helping Lindstrom, follow our trail and join us. Sandy, it's you and me, Pard. Let's ride."

"They have us by hours, Corcoran. If they follow the tracks back to Palisade they could go in any direction from there. Take the rails east or west, take the roads north, or anywhere."

"Yeah, I know. They could hole up at any of a dozen ranches, even hole up at Raines or Blackburn. At least we know who they are and what they look like. Dupree will take his anger out on anyone or anything, I'm afraid."

The rail line followed the main road, so the ride north was fairly easy and the two made good time. "We'll run out of daylight a long time before we reach Palisade," Corcoran said. "Looks like these boys we're following aren't in that big of a rush."

"Nope, they ain't worried about being followed. Cut

the wires, you see. Even Palisade doesn't know about the wreck or that these boys are heading their way. We'll come to the Vandoren place first, Corcoran."

"Well, he's a tough old bird. Won't take nothing from anyone. Just hope he sees that they might be a problem."

CHAPTER EIGHT

"That little bastard at the bank is responsible for this," Dupree said. "He set you up, Owens. Telling you he knew the schedules. I'll rip him to pieces if I ever see him again. I ought to shoot you," he screamed.

"You can try anytime you want to die," Oscar Owens growled, his right hand close to that big Colt at his side. "Somebody knew about us, and we've been bested, Dupree." He sat back on his haunches, scowling at the heavy man. He knew it would be a fight just to get north to Palisade, and then luck would have to riding high on his shoulders to get him safely out of the area.

"We're broke, gonna be hungry before long, and many miles from anywhere. We rode away from the train wreck leaving the pack animals, Dupree. You know, the ones with food and bedrolls? You want to start a fight or ride north? Your choice," Owens stood quiet, watching the big man. Dupree had a quick temper but he also had brains. He knew Owens was faster and settled down.

Despite all that trick gun shooting at the Bonanza Club, Owens knew he was far faster at pulling iron than Dupree. Dupree was a crack shot but often bungled his draw. Owens was tired of running, wanted this one big hit, a warm beach somewhere in Mexico, and a lovely lady's arms wrapped around him. If the only way he could get that was to shoot Dupree, well, that's the way the cards were dealt. Dupree must have read that in Owens' eyes and backed off.

"We've lost half a day. Can't be in Palisade before tomorrow. Let's find us a ranch, make nice with the people, get fed well, and sleep warm." The tension eased and both men relaxed.

"Kinkaid, don't never tell anyone you're a dynamite man." Dupree found himself almost laughing at the thought of that locomotive coming completely off the ground before it blew up. "I told you that fuse was too long."

"Got the train stopped," is all he said. The reality of finding no money was starting to set in and Kinkaid didn't like that at all. "We got the Cueball killed, spent days setting this up, and now we're cold and broke in the middle of damn nowhere. All because of that damn kid at the bank. He probably got some kind of ree-ward," he snickered.

"There'll be ranches all along the road, Dupree," Owens said. "There will also be buckaroos at all of them, and they don't generally welcome strangers. The herds are down from summer range and so are the cowboys. We need to be on our best behavior. Our three guns won't stack up against a bunkhouse full of cowboys."

Cold wind drove into the men's faces as they mounted up and rode north through the rest of the afternoon. "Haven't seen the first sign of a ranch, Owens. It'll be dark in a couple of hours." Dupree's anger was building, Owens could feel his own, as well. Kinkaid had stopped talking some time before.

"Bound to be one soon," Owens said. "This is all open range country and ain't much use for fences out here. Watch for a stand of trees off in this good grass and brush, near the rises."

It was Kinkaid who spotted some smoke far in the distance and they picked up the pace. "Maybe you better do the talking, Owens. I might just shoot first." Owens wasn't sure Dupree was just kidding as they turned off the main road onto the lane leading back a mile or so to the ranch house. Cattle were spread around and a few men could be seen around the buildings.

"Nice and slow and friendly," Owens said. "There're guns we can't see already aimed at us." As they neared the small two-story house, two men stepped from around the side, rifles in hand.

"What's your business?" one of them said. He was tall and lean, bronzed from spending most of his life in the saddle, and carried his rifle with a casual air of competency.

"Howdy," Owens said. "Thought we'd make better time, but one horse come up some lame. Got room in your barn for three cold travelers?" He had a sad look on his face, and a smile in his voice, and hoped like hell they would find welcome.

"Don't look like you're much prepared for a long journey to me," the big man said. "Maybe it'd be best if you just rode on. Blackburn's up the road a piece. Sleep there. Don't want no trouble," he said, and the rifle, cradled comfortably said the rest.

"Now damn it, we're cold and hungry, and just asking for a bit of kindness. Lame horse slowed us down. We ain't looking for trouble." Dupree spat it out and started to get down from his horse.

"Don't!" The big man let the barrel of the rifle come to bear on Dupree, and the outlaw stopped instantly but made for his sidearm. The buckaroo was fast as lightning, firing that rifle twice, putting two slugs through Dupree's heart before he cleared leather. Owens spun his horse and put spurs deep in its sides, leaning as low into the hors's neck as he could get.

He heard the bullet pass over his head, just inches above, and felt the horse shudder as the bullet smashed its way through skull and brain. He and the horse tumbled to the ground and before Owens could get to his feet, a rifle butt to the back of his head put him face down in the mud.

Kinkaid wasn't fast, saw Dupree get flung back off his horse, watched Owens make a break for it and crash to the ground, and saw the wrong end of a rifle aimed at his right eye. "Climb down, stranger, nice and slow." Kinkaid did. "Unbuckle that gun belt, one-handed, and slow." The buckaroo's voice was low and gravelly and filled with hate and anger.

The second cowboy was standing over Owens as he tried to get back to his feet. The man was heavy and tall, wore a massive mustache, and had his rifle in Owens's ribs. "Pull that gun nice and slow," he growled. Owens was on his feet, slipped the revolver from its holster and dropped it in the mud.

They had seen two men with rifles come around the building. Now, they saw more than half a dozen armed men standing around, waiting for someone to make the wrong move. "Where do you want 'em, Mr.

Vandoren?"

Vandoren was pushing Kinkaid away from his horse and toward Dupree's body. "Bring him over here, Fagan. These two need to dig a hole for the dead one." Vandoren turned to the barn and hollered out for Slim Carson to bring a pick and shovel. "Why do these things always happen at supper?" He stomped up the stairs to the porch and hollered for his wife to come out.

"Keep that stew hot, Brenda. Gonna be awhile before we can come in. Guess we'll have to feed the two live ones," he snickered. "Shoulda just shot 'em all, damn it. Who do you suppose they are, Sam?"

"Guess we'll have to ask 'em," Sam Fagan muttered. He and Slim Carson nudged the two outlaws to carry Dupree's body off to where a little fenced area already had some grave markers.

"No, no, Sam. Put him out and away from our family plot. Don't want it dirtied up with some creature that's got bad blood. After you get him buried, bring those two up to the house. Need some answers."

The ground was rocky and frozen, and that made it difficult to dig the grave. Owens' head hurt bad and he had wrenched his arm when he and the horse fell. He knew better than to complain and was trying to figure out how to get out of this pickle. The two cowboys never got close enough for him to swing the pick in their direction.

Kinkaid was getting slower and slower with the shovel and one of the cowboys moved to push him some and Owens sprung at him with the pick, almost tearing the man's head off. The other cowboy moved to help his partner and Kinkaid whacked him across the face with the shovel. Owens grabbed a rifle and pistol, Kinkaid did the same, and they sprinted for the barn where they knew their horses had been put up.

The rancher and his hands had gone into the house for supper and were surprised to hear two horses clatter down the lane toward the main road. It was a free-for-all getting out the door. A few shots were taken at the fleeing outlaws and Eric Vandoren ran to where the men were supposed to be burying Dupree.

"Oh, my God," he moaned, seeing Fagan's head split open with the pick. Slim Carson's face was smashed and bleeding but he was alive. "Get the horses, boys. We gonna have a lynching." Vandoren took one more look at Fagan and strode to the barn to saddle up. He and four buckaroos were riding hard for the main road when they spotted two riders about a mile off to the south.

"There they are," he shouted. "I want those bastards alive, boys. Beat the tar out of 'em, that's okay, but don't kill 'em." Pounding hooves and screams of attacking riders filled the air, and the men swarmed toward the two riders.

"What the hell is that coming toward us, Corcoran? Sounds like the whole Sioux Nation riding down on us."

"Open your coat wide, McAuliff, so they can see our badges. I think Owens and company were here before us." The two walked their horses, holding their jackets wide open so the advancing riders could see they were lawmen.

Eric Vandoren was the first to get there and pulled his horse to a sliding stop. "That you, Corcoran? You're late. Don't know who those yahoos were, but two of my best men are dead. We're gonna hang 'em."

"We're chasing three men that blew up the train and killed the engineer and fireman," Corcoran said. He briefly described the three and Vandoren said they were the ones who killed his men.

"Only two of 'em, now, though," he snickered. "I killed the burly one. We're wasting time, Corcoran. Let's ride."

"We'll get them, Vandoren. You and your men go on back home and take care of the dead. There's another deputy following along behind us some. Tell him to follow our trail if you spot him. Don't you fret none, Eric. We'll get these two." Corcoran nodded at McAuliff and they rode off.

Vandoren was sputtering mad but didn't follow. "He's right, boys. Let's bury our dead and let Corcoran do his job."

"Where we going?" Kinkaid was riding harder than he had in his life, looking back about every five seconds or so, knowing he'd see a gang of riders coming up behind them.

"North," is all Owens said. His head, shoulders, and chest hurt like the devil but he knew it would be death if he stopped. "We'll ride until it's so dark we can't see the road, Kinkaid, and if we're lucky, we'll get to see one more sunrise."

"Why'd Dupree do that? I thought we were supposed to be all friendly like?"

"Cuz he's stupid, Joey. Dead stupid." They drove their horses at a full out gallop until they had to pull them up or kill them. "Look for a stand of trees somewhere. Usually means water nearby. We're leaving a trail a blind man could follow, but we need to get hidden somewhere for the night. We'll keep going until we can't see the road."

Oscar Owens was jabbering, he knew, but it helped him think and right now, he needed to think. Joey

Kinkaid was more stupid than Jimmy the Cueball, so if they were going to live through this, it would be up to him. Find some trees and water, get hidden for the night, and do some serious planning.

He knew Palisade was north on this road, and that's all he knew. Palisade was on the Intercontinental Railroad and since they had cut the telegraph lines before blowing up the train, there might not be a welcoming committee waiting for them. *I gotta ditch this kid. He's not smart enough to get out of his own way. I got a bottle in my saddlebags. Maybe I'll let him drink it all, if he wants, and slip out and be gone.*

As the day turned to dusk, the temperature fell fast, and the bitter cold of the high desert drove right through their heavy coats. "Let's get off the road, Joey. That looks like a line of trees off to our west. Gotta be water close by."

The trees he was looking at lined the banks of Pine Creek, a sometimes running creek, but this late in the season, was just puddles here and there. There was wood for a fire, and grass for the horses, though, and just about five miles away. They rode cross-country toward the trees as it got darker and darker, colder and colder.

"Get a hole dug and pile rocks around it, Joey, and maybe we can keep that fire out of sight. I'll get wood.

Those boys will be riding hard but now that it's dark, they won't be able to see our tracks. Might just ride right on by us."

"We're gonna run out of light, Corcoran well before we run up on those jaspers. Got a plan?"

"Yup," he said with a chuckle. "Find someplace to bed down. I think we ought to ride well into the dark, Sandy. We might just get lucky and spot a fire. Ride slow, at a walk, won't hurt the horses that way."

"I been up this way a lot," McAuliff said. "We'll be coming up on Pine Creek in the next hour or so. Good place to make camp."

"Yup. For us and them. I've been through this country a lot lately chasing that damn rustling gang. Good hunting along that creek bed. More than one rustling outfit's used it, too." The chatter went on for some time as they moved north along the well-used trail.

They spotted the line of trees where the creek was and rode toward them, through a night that held millions of stars giving just enough light to keep them from riding into trouble. Trees, standing and down, jumbled rocks, and a trickle of water in the creek bed offered them a good campsite. "No fire, Sandy, but let's search for one. Cold water, cold meat, and cold biscuits will have to do tonight."

"Those boys can't be that far in front of us, Terrence, and if they have half a brain they're camped along this creek as well."

"What I'm more worried about is Amos White. He should be several hours behind us. Hopefully, Eric Vandoren will put him up for the night. I don't think he'd try to ride all night. He'd pass us right up. We'll need that gun of his."

CHAPTER NINE

"Wake up, Sandy." Corcoran shook the old tracker gently. "Think I've spotted our quail. Stay quiet." He moved back so McAuliff could climb out of his bedroll and get his boots on. "Somebody's got a fire going about a mile down from us."

"Whew, it's a cold one this morning. Wish we had a fire."

"We'll have one when we join our friends," Corcoran snickered. "Let's leave the horses and see who's getting warm up there."

They broke camp and packed the horses but left them tied off. "If we need to leave in a hurry, they'll be ready to go. We'll walk them about halfway, but we'll have to leave them. Just too noisy," Corcoran said.

Downed trees and limbs from willow, aspen, and cottonwood, clumps of grass frozen in ice and snow, and other creekside debris made it difficult for the two men to be quiet. They stayed separated and Corcoran tried his best to step in McAuliff's tracks as they made their way down the creek. There was a wide patch of open ground between the creek bank and the outlaw's campsite, but as they approached the fire, it appeared they hadn't been seen or heard.

Corcoran motioned McAuliff to stay back in the bushes and cover him as he slowly advanced on a single person wrapped in a bedroll. It took just one quick look for Corcoran to call the old man in. "We'll be tracking just one, Sandy."

"This is the one they call Joey. Oscar Owens must not have liked the kid much." Sandy McAuliff was looking at the bashed-in skull of Joey Kinkaid, and the heavy, blood-covered rock that caused the wound. "The fire's burning hot, and that tells me that Owens killed the kid less than an hour ago."

"Yup, and built up that fire so it would be spotted bringing us in. Find Owens' trail, Sandy while I run back for the horses. Glad now we brought 'em halfway."

"He's a wily devil, this Owens character," McAuliff said. "He lit that fire thinking we'd take time to bury his partner, giving him more time to run. Wily. He's on his own now, which will make our job that much harder. Has the kid's horse, too. That'll give him a fresh horse every day. Since the storm is so recent, at least we'll have a good trail to follow."

"Good," Corcoran said. "Let's ride."

"Gettin' dark, old man," Amos White muttered to his horse. "Better find us a nice spot to camp." He rode to a stand of cottonwood trees and made up a quick camp. His horse had carried himself and the railroad conductor back to Eureka where he made his report to Lindstrom and had gotten right back on the trail.

"We've had us a day, old man," he muttered, brushing the tired horse down. "We need to be back on the trail before it gets light. Hope Corcoran and McAuliff stay on it or leave some kind of sign."

The night was cold but White had a good fire going, slept hard, and was in the saddle well before sun up. The wind blew all night but there was no new snow and the trail left by yesterday's riders was plain to see.

White's family had ranched in the Diamond Valley, Amos grew up along this main road from Palisade to Eureka. "Outlaws don't know this country like I do," he muttered more than once when he spotted areas where they could have moved off the main road and onto game or Indian trails and been deep in the mountains and safe from those following.

"We'll be at the Vandoren place soon, old man. I'll

get you a good bucket of oats from old Eric. He's a crusty old guy but he runs a good operation." Amos White rode onto the Eric Vandoren ranch about an hour after sunlight only to face half a dozen rifles aimed right at him. "I'm Deputy Sheriff Amos White, "he called out.

"Show that badge, boy, nice and slow," one of the Vandoren hands hollered back. "We're not too tired to bury one more."

"It's all right, Buster, I know him," Vandoren said, stepping out from the barn. "Hello, Amos. So, you're riding for Corcoran now, eh? That be good for Corcoran. Them varmints were here yesterday, killed two of my hands. Corcoran and Sandy McAuliff are on their tail. If you ride straight for Raines, you're bound to meet up with 'em.

"You need anything?" Eric Vandoren wanted to ride with White but wasn't about to ask.

"Let me get a little grain for this old boy and you can tell me what happened," Amos White said. They walked into the barn and Vandoren put a feed sack on the horse and invited Amos to sit with him while he told about the previous day. Amos White could see the anger and frustration, and the loss that Vandoren felt.

"Those boys are mean and ugly, Eric. Their posters tell of murder and theft from Denver to right here.

Corcoran's about the toughest man I've ever known, so if I want to get in on the capture, I'd best be on my way. Thanks for the grain."

The morning sun felt good as White rode north. There hadn't been any traffic on the road since the outlaws followed by the posse laid down their tracks, and Amos could see them plainly. "Should come to Pine Creek and then Alpha in an hour or so," he muttered. He saw where Corcoran and McAuliff moved off the road toward the creek, followed them in, and then north to the outlaw camp to Joey Kinkaid's body.

"Alpha's five miles or so north, and the next railroad stop would be Blackburn. I wonder how much of the area this man Owens knows? There's people living at the Alpha station, and a few at Blackburn." He mounted up and put the horse in a solid trot, hoping to learn something when he reached Alpha.

The little town had hopes of being the main terminal on the Eureka and Palisade Line, but Eureka took those honors and the village was just a water stop now, and every train didn't stop. There were a couple of small businesses, the leftovers of a hotel, not quite rotted away, yet, and a saloon. Amos White followed Corcoran's trail right down the main street. There had been enough local traffic that the tracks got messed up.

The cobbler's shop and blacksmith were closed as he rode by and found the saloon closed as well. Amos White rode right through the village and found Corcoran's trail clear as a picture on the other side. "Thank you for the very distinct sets of track," Amos muttered. The day was warming nicely, which of course melted the snow and ice and before long he was riding in mud. "These are almost fresh prints, old man," he said to his horse. "We'll be seeing something soon. Hope I'm not riding into an ambush."

"Sorry, Joey," Oscar Owens muttered. He dropped the bloody rock, built up the fire so it would be seen, saddled his horse, and leading Kinkaid's horse, rode north out of camp. He spent hours working out how to live the rest of his life the way he wanted. He would make sure this would be his last time running away. He could almost feel tropical breezes gently cooling him despite the bitter cold of the early morning. "No more partners, no more working with anyone but me," he muttered.

"One more bank job, and a long ride to Mexico," he smiled. "I need to put miles between Eureka and that next job, miles between me and whoever might be following. Damn you, Dupree. All you had to do was be nice one time in your life."

He was surprised when he rode up on the village of Alpha. "Whoa up, there," he said to his horse. He knew there would be water and wood stops on the rail line but he didn't expect a village. It was early, there were no people visible, only a few buildings had smoke coming from their stacks and chimneys, and he rode slowly through.

A resident walked out the back door of his cabin, not twenty yards from where Owens was, but out of sight, raised his shotgun and knocked a quail to the ground, and swung to shoot his second.

Owens' horse side-stepped, Owens dropped the lead rope on the trailing horse, put his horse in a hard run, and was out of town in a flash. He rode hard for more than half an hour until he felt safe again. "I've got to get off this main road. My God, I could have ridden right into a damn sheriff or something." The railroad ran alongside the main road and Owens knew he would ride into another water stop if he kept going. "I'm leaving a trail a dead man could follow." He made up his mind that he would take the next side trail he found leading off to the west.

"Coming up on Alpha, Terrence. Think that fool would stop?"

"Not if he has half a brain," Corcoran chuckled.

They followed his tracks right through town and saw where he kicked his horse up into a run. "Something scared him. Owens doesn't know this country, McAuliff."

"Whatever scared him made him let loose of Kinkaid's horse. There it is over there by the blacksmith's. He'll be riding fast, Corcoran."

"That gang of rustlers is working this area and I'm still wondering if the bank gang and cattle gang are one and the same."

"Wouldn't make sense to me," McAuliff said. "We have company, Corcoran. Rider back about a mile, coming on hard."

"Let's get off the road and into those trees." They drove their horses into a stand of willows and cottonwoods and waited for the visitor. "Let him get past us then we'll ride out behind."

Amos White saw the two ride into the trees and had to chuckle. "Bet it was McAuliff that spotted me. That old man has eyes behind his head." He rode to where the two moved to the trees and followed them in. "Corcoran, McAuliff, it's Amos White," he hollered, riding in slow and easy.

The two rode out of the trees to meet up. "Glad you made it. Owens is running hard. Let's keep riding and you can tell us your end of the story."

"The only thing I can tell you for sure is Owens doesn't know where he is. He's just following the road, the rail line. Blackburn is right in front of us and then the Raines Ranch, the last water stop before Palisade. If he makes it all the way to Palisade, we might lose him."

"He ain't making it that far," Sandy McAuliff snarled. "Nope, he ain't."

They were riding through mud now, most of the ice and snow had melted in the midday sun. With no wind, it was a pleasant early winter ride through the long valley. "Looks like he's taking a trail off to the west," McAuliff said. "Know where that goes, Mr. White?"

"He'll be riding into the Cortez Mountains, Sandy. Lots of canyons, lots of rocks. There are a few smaller ranches back to our south. There's a couple of mines way up high. Small trails lead north to Palisade. He'd have to know the country to find them."

"Or just be dumb lucky," Corcoran said. "This is where I've been searching for those rustlers. Where would you hide some cattle in order to re-brand them?"

"Any of a half-dozen little closed canyons. They all have water and grass. Easy to make a brush fence," Amos White said. "Usually a creek will be running out from the canyon. That's the giveaway."

CHAPTER TEN

"Looks to be alone, but he's not trailing a horse. No pack animal. Might be one of those deputies been riding through the country." Freddie Camacho handed the telescope to Silas Arnold. Arnold and his brother, Bad Eye, had about fifty head of steers tucked back in the canyon, using their running irons on cattle from up and down the long valley. The three men planned to drive the small herd to the Blackburn Station in a week or so, and ship them west. That was Bad Eye's job, making the arrangements at Blackburn Station.

It's easy enough on the open range of Nevada's high mountain deserts to steal the cattle, but rebranding and finding less than particular buyers was difficult. There were others in the little gang but not with Silas Arnold today.

"Bad timing, Freddie. If he keeps coming, he'll spot

that canyon sure as hell. Kill him quietly. Too damn many people around here."

"Knife is always best, Silas. Meet you back at the fire." He stepped off his horse and tied it off to some brush as Silas Arnold turned and rode back into the deep and narrow canyon. Camacho was about five feet five, thin as a rail, dark-complexioned, and with a vivid scar across his thin face. He worked down through the rocks until he was on top of an outcrop the trail was forced to work around.

Oscar Owens was walking his horse, and as he made the circle around the large outcrop, a heavy boulder knocked him out of the saddle. His head bleeding heavily, he was trying to get to his feet, wiping blood from his eyes, and feeling tremendous pain in his shoulder from the impact when Camacho came at him with a big knife.

Owens rolled out of the way of the attack and drew his pistol, shooting the Mexican in the leg. He jumped to his feet and was about to put the killing slug through Camacho's head when another voice, just behind him, told him to "Drop the gun or die." Owens slowly let the pistol drop and turned to face Bad Eye Arnold.

"You gonna die on me, Freddie?" Arnold called out.

"No. Bullet went right on through. Bastard's quick, Bad Eye, watch him. Don't know if he was following our trail or just happened along."

Bad Eye Arnold, Silas's younger brother, wore a patch over his left eye after he lost the eye in a saloon fight years ago. He never saw a doctor after the eye was gouged out, and he's had problems with the wound ever since. "All right, who are you?" He aimed his weapon at Owens and stepped toward the outlaw.

Owens whipped out a knife from his belt and slashed Bad Eye across the face, grabbed the rustler's pistol before it hit the ground, whirled, and killed Freddie Camacho with a single shot through the chest. Arnold was on the ground, writhing in pain, his face half peeled off, blood spilling onto the ice and mud.

"The better question is, who are you?" Owens said, giving Arnold a kick in the ribs. "Come on, now, up on your feet." He moved over and picked up his own weapon, grabbed Camacho's knife, and took hold of his horse's reins. "You boys have bad attitudes and I don't much care for bad attitudes. Better tell me who you are and I mean now," and he fired a shot at Arnold's feet.

The knife had slashed across the rustler's face such that both lips were sliced at the center mark and Arnold was unable to speak, just make noise from his throat. Owens had to turn away from the sight. He tucked Camacho's knife in his belt next to Arnold's pistol and mounted his horse. "Next time I see you, you're a dead man," Owens said, and rode off down the trail at a full run.

Don't know what that was all about but if they have friends I gotta get out of here, pronto. He pushed the horse as hard as it would run, didn't see the tracks leading into the closed canyon, didn't see dust from a rider coming hard out of the canyon. Silas Arnold heard the gunshots, knew Freddie Camacho was going after the stranger with his knife and was riding to help.

"Gunshot," Corcoran said. All three sat straight up at the sound. "Not even a mile up that way." They put their horses into a strong lope following the trail through massive rock formations, around outcrops, and through dips filled with mud. It wasn't but a couple of minutes later that they heard another single shot.

"A hunter, you suppose?" Amos White asked. "Right time of the year. Doesn't sound like a gunfight or someone moving cattle."

They rode around a large outcrop to find Bad Eye Arnold on the ground, moaning in pain. Off to the side was Freddie Camacho's body, bled out. Corcoran bailed off his horse followed by Amos White. Both men handed Sandy McAuliff their reins. "This one's been cut up bad," Corcoran said, getting Arnold to take his hands from his face.

"This one's dead, shot in the leg and bled to death, I guess. Corcoran. Kind of interesting, eh? We heard two distinct shots, many minutes apart, and this guy has a leg wound. One wound." Because of the mud, he couldn't see the kill shot to the chest.

"Even more interesting, Amos, this guy doesn't have a gun," Corcoran chuckled.

"And this guy doesn't have a knife," Amos White answered back.

"Looks like Mr. Owens didn't much care for these two gentlemen," Sandy McAuliff snickered. "We've got company coming, boys, and he's riding fast." McAuliff moved the horses back around the outcrop, dismounted and tied them off to some rocks. He grabbed his rifle out of the scabbard and scampered back into some bushes.

Corcoran and Amos White jumped into the jumbled rocks at the base of the outcrop to await the visitor. They could hear the drumming hoofbeats well before they saw the single rider come up to where Bad Eye Arnold was crouched in the mud. Silas Arnold slid his horse to a stop and jumped off, running to his brother's side.

Corcoran ran to the scene as well, and with his pistol drawn, told Arnold to stop where he was. Arnold turned as if to draw, and Corcoran slapped him across the side of the head with his pistol. "No, no, buster, that's as far as you go." He disarmed Silas Arnold and rolled him over on his back. "Anyone recognize him?"

"Yeah, I sure do," Amos White said. "That's Silas Arnold. He used to steal cattle from my dad when I was a kid. When did they let you out, Arnold?" He looked at the two others and shook his head. "That might be Arnold's brother, but it's hard to say. Don't recognize the Mexican.

"Arnold ran a gang of rustlers about ten years ago, Corcoran, and our ranch was hit many times. I bet if we follow his trail back you'll find some mixed-brand cattle and maybe other members of the Arnold gang."

"All of this puts us in one hell of a mess, Corcoran," Sandy McAuliff chuckled. "Want to watch you work your way out of this one."

"And with your generous help, I will," Corcoran said. "Better get a fire lit, Sandy. I'm gonna need some brandy-laced coffee while I work this out. Got a dead one, a wounded one, and one that needs to be in irons. Got a possible herd of stolen cattle that needs to be driven out, and we got a killer running away from us. Best part, Mr. McAuliff, there are only three of us."

"Coffee and brandy comin' up, Sheriff," McAuliff chuckled. He nodded to Amos White to tie up Silas

Arnold and gathered wood for a fire. "I might have a couple of ideas after we hear yours, Corcoran."

"I was hoping so," Corcoran moved Bad Eye Arnold near the fire and Amos White got Silas Arnold seated close too. "We need to know how many men are up the canyon with the rustled cattle first. That is the most important part of my plan." He looked at Amos White and smiled. "You've run cattle and hunted in these mountains, Amos. Follow this yahoo's tracks back and see what you can see, and get back here quick."

Amos was mounted and gone in a minute. "Now, Mr. McAuliff, your job is to ride back to Alpha. That's a regular Eureka and Palisade Station so they should have a telegraph. Send wires to Palisade and Eureka about Owens. We gotta nail that killer dog down. After you do that, ride like the wind to the Vandoren ranch and bring a load of buckaroos back to drive these cattle back to Alpha."

"I can do that, Corcoran. We'll take 'em to Blackburn, though. What are you and Amos gonna be doing?"

"On the wire you send to Palisade, Sandy, I want you to instruct the resident deputy to send two people south to meet up with us. Amos and I will be bringing the prisoners north and they can take them the rest of the way. We'll meet back with you here and we'll track down Oscar Owens."

"I sure can't think of anything that would work better, Corcoran. Damnation and all that, I can't," McAuliff laughed. He mounted up and rode for Alpha.

Corcoran spent time trying to doctor Bad Eye, getting a lot of bad mouth from Silas Arnold. "You been pulling cattle from the Raines' Ranch, from old man Vandoren, and half a dozen others, Arnold. Probably got some of Hank Whipple's beef in there, too. Looks like those days are over. You ain't got no rights, mister, except for one. The right to spend the rest of your life in prison." He kicked dirt at the man. "Or hang, whichever comes first."

Amos White was back within the hour, riding in nice and slow, letting Corcoran know who it was. "Don't be shootin' me, Corcoran," he hollered out. He stepped off his horse and tied it off. He trailed two other horses. "Ain't nobody else up that canyon but cattle, runnin' irons, and more cattle. Must have fifty head or more. I saw four separate brands they were planning to alter."

"Good work. Glad you brought those horses, too. Let's get these yahoos moved into that canyon, get 'em doctored as much as we can, and wait for our boys from Palisade and Vandoren's buckaroos. Sure would rather be chasing Owens."

"Why don't you? These two ain't gonna give me no trouble. Get on his trail while it's still hot, Corcoran."

"I just hate to leave you like this." Corcoran was twisted, had obligations in three directions, but knew that catching Oscar Owens had to be number one. "All right," he said. "Keep those boys tied tight, whup on 'em all you want, and you and Sandy follow me as soon as everyone gets here."

He jumped on Dude and set the spurs lightly. All Amos White saw was dust as Corcoran headed out of the deep canyon. "He didn't need much coaxing," White murmured. "Just us boys," he said to the Arnold brothers, "and I'm a nasty host."

Ain't no reason to just sit here and wait for those deputies when I can ride north and meet them. "Silas, help me get your worthless brother in that saddle, then you get saddled up, and we're riding for Blackburn. Look at me sidewise and it'll be your last look. Move it."

CHAPTER ELEVEN

Corcoran was at least three hours behind Owens and knew that hard riding was ahead of him. This ain't the time to kill old Rube. Ride steady and read the country. I've been through all this country many times and Owens has never been here. My advantage, you bank robbin' bastard. Where would I go if I was runnin' from the likes of me? He couldn't help but chuckle.

"These mountains wouldn't be my first choice, but since he is runnin' into the Cortez Mountains, I'm going to guess that he's just gonna run until I catch him. There ain't anywhere to go once you get here," he laughed.

Winter was coming on fast and the snow from that last storm was still on the ground. Corcoran knew the Cortez Range was high and rough, and when the next storm came through most of the passes would be closed by drifts of as much as twenty feet. Any cattle still on the range would probably not live, deer, elk, and antelope should already be down in the valleys, and if he didn't catch this murdering outlaw fast, they would both be caught in winter's death grip.

"There's gonna be a point on this chase when I gonna have to say, as the mining men do, it's deep enough. There's gonna be a point where my life is more important than trying to catch you, you bank robbin', train wreckin' sumbitch."

He'd been on the road since before sunrise and was watching the sun get lower and lower in the west. "Better find a good campsite, get a good night's sleep, and kill me a killer tomorrow." The night was cold and clear with stars as bright as lanterns in the high thin air. Great bands of coyotes were in full voice, and Corcoran tossed and turned in his blankets until the morning's first dim light came.

"Feels like I rode five hundred miles last night, looking into every canyon, cavern, and cave in these mountains," he grumped, trying to get wet wood to catch fire. After some obscene language, the fire kindled and Corcoran got a pot of coffee going, some smoked elk floating in the hot liquid, and two of Cindy Payton's sourdough biscuits down. The trail the outlaw and the lawman followed led them high into the Cortez Range and, Corcoran figured, it probably would drift north toward Palisade. "This boy's lost as lost can get and on a path to his grave. We'll be crossing over eight thousand feet and all it'll take is one little storm to kill us."

The highest peak in the Cortez Mountains was slightly more than nine thousand feet and that was south of where this trail would lead. "Great towering stands of naked rocks is what we'll be looking at today, Rube," he chuckled, getting the horse fitted out. He figured the only tracks that might stand out would be those of Oscar Owens. Maybe those rustlers rode up this way, but he doubted that, too.

"Too late in the season for any ranchers to still have stock up here. It's all uphill, Rube, so we'll take as many breaks as you want to take. Don't know enough about Owens. Is he a horseman? Does he know about high altitudes and lack of air? Well, old Pard, we do and if he don't, we'll just kill that train wreckin' fool."

It was a single-track trail, not fit for buggies or wagons, and Owens' tracks did stand out, despite the ice and mud. "He's staying on the trail, Rube, cuz he's lost," Corcoran laughed. Winding through rocks, scrub brush, a few pines and scattered cedar brush, he immediately spotted a change in Owens' tracks. "Horse picked up a stone bruise,." Corcoran followed carefully for another hour, noted that Owens had stopped often.

"Horse is giving him hell, old man. He's gonna hole up soon. Losing that second horse is gonna cost you."

Corcoran could see in the tracks that Owens would have to stop, have to get that rock out or be on foot. He had to get off the main trail, too, but with jumbled rocks in every direction, that was far easier to say than do. "I'm gonna leave you in some good grass, old man, and do some rock climbing." With Rube tied off, Corcoran started moving up the sides of the mountain to the south of the trail. That's where the sun had shone for two days and the snow and ice had melted, and Corcoran could move freely among the giant boulders.

Corcoran climbed to a ridge top and was moving cautiously along the north-south spine when he spotted smoke about a mile in front and well down the mountainside. It was hard going through the massive rocks and Corcoran was finally able to get within rifle range of the smoke. It was coming straight up on this windless, early afternoon from behind a stand of rocks and pine.

Corcoran could see past the smoke and far down the hill, the trail he had been on, but he couldn't see Owens or his horse. He worked his way cautiously down the side of the mountain to where he could see where the fire and Owens should be. He saw the outlaw standing next to his horse, holding one front leg up and back, and was trying to dig out a small rock wedged between the hoof and iron shoe.

Corcoran slowly made his way closer, getting to within about thirty yards of the man when a bullet smashed into a rock just inches from his head. He dove to the ground, rolled behind a boulder, rifle in hand, looking for the shooter. When Owens heard the shot, he dropped the horse's leg and dove behind a stand of rocks as well. Another shot went off, glancing off the rock Corcoran was hiding behind.

Owens took that opportunity to jump on his horse and, despite its lameness, rode down the mountain. He reached the trail and forced the horse into as fast a trot as it would go. Corcoran saw where the second shot came from and moved back from the rock he was behind and started to circle around a stand of pine trees. He saw a single man with a rifle about two hundred yards down the hill from him and recognized the man immediately.

He moved behind a large tree and cupped his hands. "Rafferty," he yelled. "Don't shoot. It's Corcoran, Terrence Corcoran you're trying to kill."

Sonny Rafferty was the foreman at the Raines' Ranch, and Corcoran watched the big man lower the rifle and stand up. "It better be you I see stepping out in the sunlight, Corcoran. I got a big anger going."

"It's me," Corcoran said, stepping out from behind the tree. "A killer just rode away because of your shooting, so I got somewhat of an anger myself." He made his way down the hillside and joined with the big buckaroo. "Why you shootin' at me?"

"Been looking for rustlers in this canyon for some time, Corcoran. Spotted tracks and followed, saw your horse, spotted you hiding in the rocks, and shot at you. Figured you were one of the rustlers."

"Damn," Corcoran said. "I got a deputy coming down from Palisade to the Raines' ranch right now because of rustlers. Two of them are dead, a third is in custody. Eric Vandoren has a crew coming north to bring the rustled steers to a railhead. Sumbitch," he almost shouted. "I was trackin' a killer and train robber, and now he's on the run again."

Corcoran ran and Rafferty trotted back down the trail to where Rube was tied off and Corcoran mounted up. "If you want to make up for this, ride with me, Rafferty."

"I'll ride with you, Corcoran, but I ain't done nothing wrong." Rafferty ran a tight ranch, didn't take anything from anyone, and wasn't about to start now, despite being a friend of Corcoran's for many years. He was tall like Corcoran but carried many extra pounds on his big frame. He tried to drink Corcoran under the table once, which culminated in the complete destruction of a small saloon.

A second fight ensued over who would pay the damages. Corcoran demanded his right to pay, and Rafferty did the same. The owner settled the matter buy buying them a fresh bottle and suggesting they drink it elsewhere.

"So, who's this bugger you're not able to catch by yourself, Corcoran?"

Oscar Owens pushed that poor horse just as far as he dared, and after an hour and a half of hard riding, finally, knew he had to give it up for the day. He was in a wide glade, a stream along one side, fair grass, cottonwood, aspen, and pine trees along the creek and across the valley. He crossed the creek into a stand of cottonwoods with the canyon wall as a backdrop and made his camp.

The trail had climbed another couple of thousand feet, Owens was near the highest ridge, and the air was thin. He and the horse were panting and tired. The only thing Owens knew for a fact, was Palisade was north of where he was, and Palisade is where he had to be.

"At least I'll be able to see 'em coming," he muttered.

He had to get that rock dislodged from the horseshoe if the horse would ever be ride-able again, and worked on that before laying out a fire pit or gathering wood. He broke the tip off his knife, cussed loud and long, and after at least half an hour of work, got the stone out. The horse kicked and fought him the entire time, and Owens was forced to take short rest periods.

He walked the horse down to the creek and let it stand in the cold water for several minutes before bringing it up to some good grass. "Get that foot well, horse. We got miles to go."

The one thing missing from his kit was food, and Owens knew that would be the end of the chase if he didn't come up with something. He knew there were men coming up the trail behind him, didn't know where he was, exactly, or how far from anywhere there might be food. He knew the trail had turned north, that he was following along near the crest of the mountain range, and hoped it would take him to Palisade.

He was gathering broken limbs from the cottonwood grove when he spotted a rangy old jackrabbit sitting near the creek. A quick shot tore half the rabbit's head off and he had meat; tough, stringy, not very tasty, meat. *Boil it and it ain't bad, but I don't got no pot. Got no pan to fry it in, and puttin' it on a stick just makes it tougher.*

He got a good fire going, pulled some coals to the side and put a thin flat rock on top of the coals. After several minutes, giving the rock time to get blistering hot, he laid sliced liver and one hind leg on the rock. *Ain't quite what I prefer.* His plan was San Francisco where he knew he would find fresh oysters, fine whiskey, and beautiful women. *I ain't never runnin' from nothing, ever again. San Francisco to fill my poke and Mexico to live out my life.* He let those thoughts take him into a hard sleep.

Corcoran spent time telling Rafferty about the botched train robbery and the chase north. "So this yahoo killed two of Vandoren's men? He's now my worst enemy, Corcoran. Next to you, of course. Bout time you caught those rustlers, too. Lost a lot of beef because of them."

"Wouldn't be losing 'em, Sonny, if you kept them home where they belong, instead of lettin' 'em run loose all over these hills. Amos White said the man we caught is called Silas Arnold. Know him?"

"I know of him. Rustled the Diamond Valley years ago. Supposed to be behind bars. See? There you go, Corcoran. You tell me I shouldn't let my calves run around loose, but you law people let cattle rustlers out of jail."

The commentary went back and forth all the way to sunset. "We're going more north now, Rafferty, and Owens is trying his best to make Palisade on a crippled horse. Let's camp up and we'll catch him in the morning."

"When are your people gonna catch up with us? You said Amos White and Sandy McAuliff are coming?"

"They won't be coming together. White took the prisoners north to Blackburn and Sandy went south to Vandoren's place. We're on our own, Sonny, but we have food, that creek's running with cold water, and I just happen to have a little bottle of brandy to allow us all the comforts of a good camp."

The battle of words went back and forth as the level in the brandy bottle slowly dropped well down, and sleep came to the two with ease.

CHAPTER TWELVE

Amos White dug a shallow grave for Freddie Cama-cho, had Bad Eye Arnold tied on the saddle, his horse's lead rope tied to Silas Arnold's. Bad Eye was more unconscious than awake, but Silas was fully awake and angry at being tied up like a hog. They were several miles out of Blackburn and would be there well before sunset.

"When my boys have found out what you've done to my brother, they'll slice you up like a side of bacon, Amos White."

"You ain't got no boys, Arnold," Amos snickered. " You not only got no gang, you got no rustled cattle. All you got is knowin' you're goin' back to prison. More likely a gallows."

They rode at a walk and all the time Silas Arnold was trying to work his hands loose from the tight rope.

White had done a good job of tying him off and he couldn't get free. His hands were drawn back behind him, then crossed before being tied. The end of the rope was then looped around his waist and tied off again. Arnold had drawn blood he was fighting so hard.

"We gotta stop," Silas Arnold said as Blackburn came in to sight. "I gotta pee, bad."

"We'll be in town shortly," White chortled. He was glad to see there were horses tied near the water tanks. Blackburn was going to be a major stop along the Eureka and Palisade rail line, but it never developed. There were a few people living in the immediate area, but not what the planners had expected. Cattlemen built chutes for loading the steers for rides to market.

"My relief column should be waiting for us, Arnold," he joked. "After I turn you over to them, you can pee to your heart's delight. You're a lucky man that it's me bringing you in. If it was Eric Vandoren or one of the other ranchers, you'd already be dead. Hangin' from a high cottonwood, my friend. Yup, a lucky man." He had to chuckle listening to the ugly words that were spat his way.

"When I was just a boy and listened to my father complain about you stealin' our cattle, I wanted to catch you, torture you, make you scream in terror, Silas Arnold. And, just looky here, I gotcha all tied up and cryin' like a baby cuz you gotta pee. I love torture, Silas Arnold." Amos couldn't help but chuckle when Arnold spent more than a minute cussing at him.

"There's two kinds of torture, Arnold. Did you know that? Yup, the physical, where you get ripped and shredded, and the psychological, where a mean old deputy sheriff won't stop so you can pee." The cussing continued for another full minute, along with some laughter, of course.

They rode past a couple of abandoned buildings, passed by a few that were occupied, big eyes peering through dirty windows, and rode up to the rail company yards. The deputies from Palisade were waiting for him along with two other men. "Glad you made it, Toby. I've had my fill of the Arnold brothers. Who's that with you?" Two big buckaroos had their backs to him.

Toby Smith waved hello and walked up to take the lead ropes from Amos. Smith was the resident deputy in Palisade, and his deputy, Jenkins, was getting Bad Eye Arnold untied and off the horse. "The big man on the left is Hank Whipple from the Rocking W, and the other is Jonas Holiday, his foreman. They got the word somehow that you were bringing in the rustlers. Looks like trouble to me."

"Those people on the telegraph can't keep their

mouths shut. Trouble? Better spell it out, Toby. I've already had a lot of trouble and Corcoran is expecting me. He's on the trail of a killer right now. Whipple, eh? Haven't seen the old guy for years. My father had a ranch that neighbored his."

"I know how you feel, but this is real trouble," he said, and White could see a combination of anger and fear in Toby Smith's eyes. "I think Whipple plans to hang our prisoners."

"That ain't gonna happen." Amos White dismounted and let Smith take his horse to a hitching rack. White took his time brushing trail dust and watched as Hank Whipple and Jonas Holiday slowly walked to him.

"Glad you caught these bastards, Amos," Whipple said. "When did you go to work for the sheriff?"

"Evening, Hank. Couple of weeks now," he chuckled. "Seems like years. These fools get some of your beef, too? I saw brands from several outfits in their little cache basin."

"Yup, they did, Amos, that's why Jonas and I are here. Gonna see these bastards hanging from that water tower over there."

"Well, no, I don't think so, Hank. They're my prisoners and they'll see a judge before they get hanged up somewhere." He knew that Hank Whipple had the reputation of a man who wrote his own rules, and backed them up with firepower. The bigger problem, though, would be Jonas Holiday. The man was more outlaw than buckaroo and bragged often about how many men he had supposedly shot.

"More'n likely you got some beef in that herd Eric Vandoren will be driving in, but lots of other folks do, too. The law will handle this, Hank." Amos White stood several feet from the two burly men and had his right hand resting comfortably on his heavy Colt.

"Law can go to hell on this one, boy. Silas Arnold and that ignorant brother of his has stolen their last beef. They hang, and I mean to be doin' the hangin'. Now, Amos White, tuck that ba-ge away somewhere and let us ranchers handle the matter."

Before Amos could say anything, the sound of hoofbeats signaled the arrival of another rider. The horse slid to a stop just in front of Hank Whipple and the rider was off and running to the man. "Don't you dare let him do this," the girl said, flinging herself into Whipple's arms. She was tall and slim, and very obviously a fully developed young lady.

"You stay out of this, Helen. Go home. This doesn't concern you."

"Well, it certainly does." She almost shouted. "Those are our cattle that were stolen. Not just yours,

Papa. Mama's and mine, too. If you hang him, you'll be accused of murder and then what? Then what?" She said again, almost stomping her little foot. "Then, I'll be fatherless, that's what."

The two stood eye to eye, he, at almost six feet and near two hundred pounds, her, almost five and ten inches, weighing a whole one twenty. Amos White saw her father in her moves, her anger, but mostly, he saw her mother in her beauty.

Helen Whipple's hair was so black it was almost blue, and her naturally dark complexion was sun bronzed into a deep darkness that glowed in the late day's sun. Her mother's family had California roots that dug back into the Spanish era of the seventeen hundreds and Whipple had fallen for Esmeralda the minute he spotted her at a Spanish Fandango in Santa Barbara.

"Now, honey, ain't no judge gonna call me a murderer for hanging the likes of the Arnold brothers. He should have been hung ten years ago. Now, please, go home. Let us men take care of the problem."

She almost said it, held it back but wanted to say, you men are the problem this time. Her lips quivered, her fists were knotted up, and she turned to Amos White. White had been standing quietly, his mouth open, his eyes filled with Helen Whipple. "Do something," she almost shouted. "Don't just stand there with your mouth open. You're wearing a badge, do something."

Jonas Holiday started to take her by the shoulders to her horse and she spun free. "Don't you put your murdering hands on me. It's your fault my father is mixed up in this." She stood in front of Holiday and he again tried to take her to her horse. She slapped him hard across the face and he smashed her in the mouth with a gloved fist, knocking her to the ground.

Amos White took one step and sent a crushing right fist to Holiday's head, sending the man headfirst into the mud, alongside Helen. He jerked his revolver as Holiday went for his and fired a single shot into the man's upper torso, to his left, making the man's right arm go limp. He turned quickly and held the gun dead aimed at Whipple's heart.

"Take your man and your daughter and go home, Whipple. The law will see to it that these men will go to trial for their crimes. Don't make this any worse than it already is. Your daughter is covered in mud, your man is wounded, and your beef is safe, go home. That's where you belong."

Whipple hadn't seen a man draw a weapon as fast as Amos White had, actually saw the man adjust his aim so as not to kill Holiday. He helped Helen to her feet and she twisted away from him, and then he tried to get Jonas Holiday up and out of the mud.

"I told you to bring the crew to hang those bastards, Hank. Maybe next time you'll listen to me," Jonas Holiday said through clenched teeth. Amos White noticed immediately that Helen was not helping to doctor Holiday, but was concerned for her father.

"No, Papa, you're doing right. Your lust for blood, Mr. Holiday, almost cost my father his freedom. We'll go home, and Deputy White will bring our cattle home." She looked over at Amos and smiled, almost buckling Amos's knees. She giggled and turned back to her father. "Those Outlaws will stand trial and probably hang, or at least spend the rest of their lives in prison. Come," she said, "let's go home."

She looked over at Amos and smiled, again. This time his knees weakened visibly. *She was a skinny little brat last time I saw her. My God.* There were so many things he wanted to say, like, It's very nice to see you again, or, you're such a lovely lady, or, or. *Damn it, if I was Corcoran I'd be chatting her up, she'd give me a kiss on the cheek.*

"Holiday's hurt, Miss Helen, but he should make the ride home without trouble. It's nice to see you again." Amos choked the words out. He was looking at the ground that separated them and heard her giggle just a bit.

"Thank you, Amos. You've grown up, too. I won't kick mud on your shiny boots," she said. She was on her horse, riding alongside her father as he led the three out of the rail yard. The memory of that little twit kicking mud on his new boots brought a full right-out-loud laugh from the young deputy. *Sure would love to hear some of the conversations they'll have on that ride home.*

"Good job, White," Toby Smith said. "Think that old bastard will trail us and try to hang these boys?"

"His fight's over. Holiday couldn't no matter how much he might want to follow, and Helen will see to it that nothing else happens. Her mother, Esmeralda Whipple will probably have some strong words, too, when they get home."

"You could have killed that man, Amos. I saw you pull off. Why?"

"Not the time for killin', Toby. Holiday's got a mean and stupid outlook on life and he will die hard someday, but this wasn't the day. I was stoppin' a killin'. It's hard to explain, but killing an outlaw has to be the final decision, not the first." He stopped talking, thinking he was just talking in circles.

Sure, I could have killed Holiday, and damn right, he was gonna try to kill me, but his crime, bashing Helen, wasn't a killing crime. I think sometimes I think too much. He chuckled, looking into Toby Smith's confused face. "It's gettin' late. You gonna try to get these men to Palisade tonight?"

"Was. Before you started a gunfight," he joshed. "We'll camp here in the yard and leave out at sunrise. Got plenty of food and won't have any trouble from those two. Silas's head hurts and Bad Eye is almost dead anyway. You leavin' out?"

"Gotta find Corcoran. He's trailin' that killer. Have a good ride back to Palisade." He mounted up and rode out from the rail yard, thoughts and images of little, skinny Helen Whipple dancing in his head. *She must have been ten when I was goin' to that big cook-out and dance. New boots, new hat, and she knocked my hat off and kicked dirt on my boots. Thought it was the funniest thing she'd ever done.*

So many years ago, he thought, and now he was a deputy sheriff, saved her father from doing something terrible, and shot the man that whupped on her. *It's a long ride from Eureka to the Rocking W ranch, but I'm gonna make that ride a time or two. With a new hat.* He chuckled as he rode.

"I'm not sure that what I did was right or wrong, Papa, but I am sure that what you were trying to do would have been wrong. I'm also glad that Amos shot Mr. Holiday. He's no good, Papa, and you know it."

Hank Whipple was still angry and embarrassed and didn't take kindly to being chewed out by his own daughter. "Best to be quiet, girl. Those men need hanging and you know it."

"Rustling cattle in Nevada is a hanging crime, Papa, and it's supposed to be done by the law. How many times have you lectured me on being true to the law? About the law this, and the law that."

Whipple rode quietly for some time, letting those words burn their way into his heart. She was right, he knew. He spent a lot of time seeing to it that she knew the difference between right and wrong, that laws were written to protect people from those who didn't know that difference. That most lawmen were good in their hearts and should be respected for the work they do.

"Damn it, Helen," he stammered. Holiday was slumped in his saddle and Hank and Helen were riding side by side. She was good with horses, rode well, and he was proud of her. "You're right, your mother is right for not stopping you, and I have spent too much time listening to Jonas Holiday. You did catch young Amos White's attention, eh?"

She blushed, tried to hold in a giggle, and continued looking forward. Visions of being knocked to the ground, seeing Amos whip Holiday to the ground and then shooting the man because he hit her, played in full color. "He's grown into quite a man," she almost whispered.

"Think he'll come calling?" Whipple chuckled. "Could use a man like that around this old ranch."

"I'd like that," she answered. "What are you going to do about Holiday, Papa?"

"Treat his wounds until he can be on his own and turn him out. Have to. Can't have a man around my ranch that thinks it's okay to hit my daughter. It is me who should have shot him, not some snot-nosed deputy." Whipple's anger returned that fast.

"I'm glad it was Amos White. If he does come calling remind me to kick dirt on his boots, Papa," she laughed.

CHAPTER THIRTEEN

Sandy McAuliff led Eric Vandoren and three buckaroos into the cut-off canyon where Arnold had the
rustled cattle tucked away. "Amos White said there's
about fifty of 'em back in there, Eric. Corcoran's out on
the trail trying to find that killer, so I'll be leaving you
now. Feels like another damn storm coming in."

Vandoren had driven them hard on their trek north,
fearing Arnold may have other men near-by to move
the cattle. "His brother's an imbecile, but Silas Arnold
is one cagey outlaw. He could have had men out rustling cattle and that herd could be moved before we
get there." No one tried to slow the old rancher down
and they had tired horses as they entered that closed
canyon.

"You're sure the Arnold brothers are in custody?"
Eric Vandoren asked again. "They need a good hangin,

that's what they need."

"I think when the judge looks at what they've done this time, that's what they'll get. It's not just cattle this time, there are dead men involved. Have a good ride, Eric."

"I will, and you and Corcoran bring that bastard down. I lost two good men because of him. I want to know he's dead, McAuliff."

They shook hands and Sandy McAuliff drifted back to the trail Corcoran should be on. *I might make at least a few miles before I run out of daylight. Wonder how Corcoran's doing?* No one had been on the trail since yesterday when all the carnage took place and Sandy noticed a third set of prints. *This ain't good. Somebody's tracking Terrence.* "Let's go, boy," he said, touching his horse with his spurs. *Just how many people are involved in all this?*

He found where Corcoran had tied Rube at the side of the trail, found spent cartridges on the ground a little further up, and then bootprints from two men. "Something strange goin' on," he muttered. He found where Owens had camped and used his fire pit to make a quick supper. It got dark fast and McAuliff spread his bedroll. "I miss nights like this," he muttered. The thin air made the older man tired but a kaleidoscope of stars, blazing in that same thin air made him smile. "I'm on a chase, in the mountains alone. The only thing wrong with this picture is that I smell a big storm in the works. Can't worry about something I can't do anything about." He pulled the old wool blanket around his shoulders and slept sound, waking to the sound of wind in the trees and coyotes in the distance.

"Just as I said, horse. We got a damn storm coming in." There were men in Eureka that believed Sandy McAuliff could smell them coming. Breakfast consisted of hot coffee and biscuits and he was on the trail. He was sitting just off the single-track, in the shade a couple hours later when he spotted dust well down the trail.

"Interesting," he mused. "Someone trailing Corcoran, and now, someone trailing me. I wonder if the Arnold brothers did have a small gang?" He chuckled. "Maybe Eric isn't seeing things." He moved back into the trees, slipped the Henry out of its leather, and waited for whoever was making the dust.

"Whoever was following Corcoran is now riding with him," McAuliff muttered. "I hope it's by Corcoran's choice." The rider came on at a hard trot, making good time on the rocky trail. "Well, now, looky here," McAuliff chuckled.

He rode out from the trees when Amos White was

fifty yards or so from him. He held his rifle in one
hand, high up, an old army sign of friend. "Glad you
could make the party, young man. Any problems with
the prisoners?"

"One little scuffle," White said. "Think we're close
to Corcoran? Who's he riding with?"

"Glad you spotted that, too. Don't know but we'll
know within the hour, I think. Prints we're looking at
are mighty fresh. Feel that chill in the air? We gotta get
that killer today cuz we're riding in snow tomorrow."

"This trail goes way back in time, doesn't it?"
White was looking at how deep the track was. "It's
used a little more than what we're seeing, too. Not
made by buckaroos moving their cattle through here,
and no buggies or wagons could use it." Amos White
remembered chasing deer along this trail when he was
a kid. "It's more than a game trail."

"Probably been used for hundreds of years, Amos,
lad. Shoshone and Paiute country we're in, and good
hunting country. All that country along Pine Creek,
the whole of Diamond Valley, was fine hunting country. You're right, son, this is an old trail. When I guided and tracked for the army, we'd find single tracks
like this one that were as much as eight inches deep.
Used for a thousand years or more."

They talked quietly as they rode at a trot along the

spine of the Cortez Mountains. The wind had picked up, had an icy feel to it, and McAuliff couldn't keep the idea of a big storm out of his head. *Don't like getting caught out like this in this. We're high in this range and that's dangerous.*

His thoughts were interrupted by a single gunshot, well in front of them. "Let's ride," he said, touching his spurs to his horse.

"I'd bet a whole faro table of gold that I saw movement in those trees, Corcoran. Don't scoff, I got good eyes." Sonny Rafferty had pulled his horse to a stop quickly and motioned Corcoran off the trail. They had come around a steep bend in the trail, which leveled off and ran along a creek and through a stand of mixed trees.

"Go on foot, old man? Are you that sure?"

"Yup," he said. "Wasn't game. Too big. A man on a horse, Corcoran. I'm sure." He pointed to a stand of cottonwood with a solid rock wall behind it. They moved into the trees and tied their horses in fair grass.

"Let's follow along the rock wall, not the creek. Owens' horse was limping bad yesterday, and it might still be giving him hell. He's quick, old man, so don't hesitate if we find him. He's killed several men in the last few days, including one of his partners so, no quarter."

"That's the way I like it, Corcoran. You up to this? You're puttin' on in the years, you know."

"You'll lose some of that beef you're carrying tryin' to keep up," Corcoran said, leading the way through the rocks and brush to the sheer rock wall. "Time for quiet, now, children," he chuckled. There were lots of trees and brush, tumbled rocks, and footing wasn't the best. The ice and snow may have melted in the sunlight, but the rocks were slick and turned in the mud at the slightest misstep.

Corcoran figured that whatever Rafferty had seen was about half a mile in front of them, and they made the first half of that quickly. "Easy now, big fella," he said, stopping them. "Let's get some separation. I'll move off into the trees more, and let's go slow."

They smelled the smoke before they saw the camp and came in very slow. Corcoran was separated from Rafferty by at least twenty yards as they advanced on the still-burning fire pit. What Rafferty had seen was Owens mounting his horse and riding off, leaving the fire and the remains of a half-eaten jackrabbit. They raced back for their horses, mounted and rode hard for half an hour, spotting Owens turning off the trail into another stand of cottonwood and pine trees.

Owens must have spotted them and spurred his horse into a full run through the wild country. He was going cross-country, racing around stands of trees, great pinnacles of rock, and ditches hidden by brush.

He had to pull up at a large and thick stand of pinyon pine, aspen and cottonwood trees. They were just too thick to ride through at a full run. He made another fifty yards or so and was almost blocked in. He grabbed his rifle, dismounted, and tied the horse.

Some of the pinyon forests were Nevada range over hundreds of acres and were so thick a man had trouble walking through them. The supply of nuts has been a main source of food for Paiute and Shoshone tribes for thousands of years. Unlike many in the pine tree family, pinyons grew branches out almost from the ground level. Deer have been known to get on their knees to crawl into the forests to get at the nuts or hide from hunters.

Owens moved through the trees and saw an opening, dashed to it, and found himself about to run into a small pasture and a spring-fed stream. Off to the north side stood a line shack and, on the hillside behind it, the opening of what might have been a mine. He made the hard run through tumbled rocks, brush and scrub cedar, and found the cabin door open.

He rushed inside, slammed the door and had to keep it closed with a crossbar that swung into place. There was a window next to the door, another one

on the opposite side of the cabin, and in the middle
of the one room, a small stove with some dried wood
stacked next to it. Owens rushed to the front window
and spotted Corcoran and another man running hard
toward the cabin. He brought his rifle up and fired one
round quickly.

"Damn, slow down, stupid. Shoot to kill, not scare
the bastards." Owens' first shot sailed over Corcoran's
head and he dove into the mud behind some rocks.
Rafferty moved off to the right, slipped into the heavy
forest and started working his way toward the side of
the cabin.

Corcoran rolled to his left, inched his way toward
some more rocks, and had a clear view of the cabin and
its open window. He saw where Rafferty was heading
and waited for the big buckaroo to get in position.
"Hope that big sumbitch finds a window on the other
side, or another door," Corcoran muttered. He saw a
rifle barrel poke out of the window, took a long slow
squeeze on his trigger and heard the ricochet. "Won't
be firing that one again, you train wreckin' bastard."

Oscar Owens hands stung like the devil from the shot,
his rifle was on the floor with a damaged muzzle, and
he looked quickly at the back window. "Gotta get out
of here. They'll burn me out, sure as hell." He slowly

crawled through the window, took a quick look around and made a run for what he thought might be a mine, stopping when he got into the dark cavern. It took a full minute for his eyes to adjust and he saw it was more a cave, but there were candles stuck in the walls, and a few boxes stashed along one wall.

"Ain't a mine," he murmured. "Must be some kind of storage cave. Damn strange." He moved back to the opening quickly to see if anyone had noticed his run. The heavy forest was off to his left, the cabin straight in front, and a sheer rock wall to his right. He couldn't see anyone. Corcoran was hidden from view by the line shack, and Rafferty was hidden in the trees. Neither of them had seen Owens' dash to the cave.

Owens got a couple of the candles lit and took a long look around the cavern. It was not a natural cave, had been dynamited for storage, he figured. "Ain't nobody been in that shack for a long time and it don't look like anybody's been in here, either," he muttered. "Don't make no sense to me, but I gotta get out of here.."

He knew he couldn't get out to the right. That mountain was almost straight up. "I gotta get in those trees and I gotta get back to my horse right now." He slipped out of the cavern and eased along the side of the hill toward the deep forest, trying to see anything that might kill him. He was partially hidden by brush and kept as low as he could on the hillside. It took at least ten minutes, and he found himself surrounded by aspen, pine, and cottonwood, and in their deep shadow.

"Gotta get back to my horse," was his only thought as he made his way deeper into the forest. He stopped, took a look back toward the cave and line shack, got his bearings, and started moving as quietly as possible back toward his horse. *I'm so tired of running. That bank job should have been the one to set me up. I should be on a train for San Francisco and then a boat to Mexico. Dupree's anger, that's what's gonna get me killed. That and that stinking liar of a kid at the bank.*

Corcoran would have laughed right out at the thought. He has said, thousands of times, just how stupid an outlaw can be. It would never have entered Owens' thoughts that it wasn't Dupree or Johnny Lewis who was responsible for the current situation. It was Oscar Owens' fault and only Oscar Owens' fault. "They're always quick to blame everyone around them for their own shortcomings," Corcoran has said so many times. "I love to chase dumb outlaws."

Rafferty moved through the trees until he was in a position to just walk right up to the blank side of the shack. He listened but heard nothing from inside and moved around to the front door. The window was on the other side of the door, but he couldn't get the door open. The crossbar held it solidly in place.

Rafferty stepped back from the door and motioned to Corcoran he was going to go around back to see if there was a door there, and Corcoran acknowledged his wave. Corcoran was slowly advancing on the cabin, one little rock pile at a time, and trying to get off to the side, away from that open window. He hadn't heard or seen anything since his one shot at the rifle barrel.

Corcoran kept reminding himself that Owens didn't know where he was and didn't have food or supplies. "This guy's gonna lose big time, and I'm the one taking him down," he muttered. "Blowin' up that train and killing those men is one thing. Killing his own partner is another. And killing Eric Vandoren's men is still another. Oscar Owens, I'm gonna have strips of your meat hanging to dry when this over."

He was almost ready to make his move to the side of the house when Rafferty started yelling at the back of the house. Corcoran was on his feet, running fast toward the howling. "He's gone, Corcoran. Gone. Just like that," Rafferty called out when Corcoran came around the side of the shack. "Door was open and nobody's there."

Corcoran ran to the cavern and found it empty, too.

He saw Owens' bootprints along the hillside and started following them, but stopped suddenly. "The horses, Sonny. He's making for the horses."

CHAPTER FOURTEEN

"Looks like whoever is riding with Corcoran knows this country as well as we do," Sandy McAuliff said, as they rode out from Owens' last camp. "We heard two shots, separated by several minutes, and not that far in front of us."

"One of the horses has a distinct limp, Sandy." They rode at a fast trot, the prints in the trail standing out, and really, no where else for the riders to go. That is, until they found where Owens jumped off the trail to ride cross country into the wilderness, and then was blocked by the heavy forest.

The ride cross country led them through great rock piles, stands of pine and scrub cedar, and heavy sage brush, but they were stopped at the heavy forest. The crest of the Cortez Range towered over this little rock and timber strewn hollow, and great billows of massive clouds were campaigning for their dramatic entrance. Hundreds of acres of pinyon pine so thick you couldn't ride a horse through it. "No one's riding through that mess," Amos White said. "There's Corcoran's horse, and another. Everyone's on foot."

"Guess we are, too, son," McAuliff chuckled. They were in the process of tying off their horses when they heard someone crashing through the trees. "Hit the ground."

White dropped to the ground and crawled behind a thick pine tree, searching for whoever was making all the noise. McAuliff grabbed his Henry from his horse and dropped behind a stand of rocks. "It's Owens," White hollered. Oscar Owens was running hard, ducking and fending off pine branches, coming toward the horses.

"Stop right there!" Amos White had his Colt aimed at the outlaw and Owens dove to the ground pulling his revolver and firing a shot as he hit. The bullet bounced off a rock in front of Amos White and hit him in the thigh, knocking him to the ground. Owens was hidden behind a tree and couldn't see Sandy McAuliff. He made a quick move forward and Sandy got off a quick shot, missing the man by inches.

"How bad?" McAuliff called out.

"Can't walk. Not gonna die," White yelled back.

"He's off to my right."

Owens used their banter to get a bead on exactly where the two men were and made his way quietly through the trees to the opposite side of the horses. He was within five feet of Sandy McAuliff before he even saw the man and swung that big revolver hard, smashing bone in the back of the old tracker's head, knocking him out cold. He had McAuliff's horse untied and was in the saddle at a full gallop back toward the trail before Amos White could swing around to get off a shot.

"Run," Corcoran howled when he heard the gunshots. He and Sonny Rafferty fought their way through the heavy pine forest, and saw Owens dust as they cleared the last of the trees. Corcoran spotted McAuliff face first in the mud, then White trying to crawl to Sandy's side.

"Take care of them," he yelled. "I'm riding." Corcoran was on Rube and on Owens' trail immediately. It was a hard cross-country chase through heavy brush and around rocks and trees, and he lost sight of Owens right away. "I ain't gonna kill you, Rube, but I am askin' for everything you've got, boy," he said.

Owens hit the trail and kept Sandy McAuliff's horse at a hard gallop. The wind had picked up considerably, snow was beginning to fall, and Owens needed some place to hole up.

"I gotta hole up somewhere that I can see this man coming after me. Gotta kill him and get on with it. Runnin' from place to place and never killin' that bastard ain't gonna work."

Owens jumped down, pistol in hand, and made his way into the rocks at the side of the trail. He moved as quickly as he could, getting as far off the trail as possible before looking for a place to hide.

He was near the crest of the range late in the day, and found a stand of rocks he could hide in and still see down the mountainside. The wind had been picking up throughout the day and was now nearing gale force. Black clouds, ferocious looking, towered thousands of feet over the Cortez Range and the temperature had dropped well below freezing. Great blankets of heavy snow descended on the ridge crest, obliterating the scenery. He was above eight thousand feet, high in a wilderness he had never been in, trailed by a man determined to kill him, and he felt the icy fingers of death touching his neck.

Terror would be his driving force. The terror of being this high on a mountain as a winter stormed barreled in. Terror of knowing he had no food, no bedroll, and only the ammunition in his belt. Terror of knowing the man chasing him was determined to kill him.

If Owens knew nothing else, the one thing for sure was: if he were to live, the man chasing him had to die. He thought he had no food or water, no bedroll, and limited ammunition. He stole Sandy McAuliff's horse and the saddlebags were full of food and a good bedroll was tied off. He was on the top of a mountain range that had peaks well over eight thousand feet and an early winter blizzard was imminent. "I have got to kill this man now. I need his horse, his food, and his bedroll to live through this storm."

One of the first rules of survival was to control panic and Oscar Owens had lost that battle hours ago. Two thoughts beat on each other: kill whoever was following, ride hard for Palisade and escape on the Western Pacific.

"Bullet was smashed by that rock and tore up my leg pretty bad," Amos White said. He had his pants leg ripped open showing an ugly wound. "At least it isn't bleeding that bad."

"Gotta get you off this mountain, boy, before this storm unloads on us. I told you we were in for a big one, and it's here now." Sandy McAuliff was sitting in the mud next to White, nursing his still bleeding head. He felt dizzy and nauseous. His stomach was churning, ready to unload at any moment. *We have to move now or we'll both die before morning.*

Sonny Rafferty got a fire started. "I'm gonna get you two fixed up enough to ride out of here," Rafferty said. "I gotta catch up with Corcoran. That boy sure knows how to get in a mess, don't he?"

"It's worse than that, Rafferty," McAuliff said. "Owens stole my horse and left me with a crippled and stove up wreck. Get that coffee started and I'll take care of our wounds. We're looking at a killer blizzard,. Get with Corcoran, kill Owens, and get off this mountain."

How many times had he fought his way through storms like this when he guided for the army? How many men died because some damn fool officer wouldn't listen? "I can feel it in my bones, Rafferty. This is a killer blizzard comin' down on us."

Sonny Rafferty grumbled but had lived in the Diamond Valley all his life. He knew what these massive storms looked like at valley level, not at ridge top level. Wind in the valley might be sixty some miles per hour, but up here? One hundred? One fifty? Rafferty listened to the old tracker, mounted up, saluted the gentleman, and rode off.

Sandy fought off his nausea, kept his balance, and had coffee boiling along with another pot with hot water to clean the wounds to his head and Amos's leg. "This feels like a February blizzard comin' down on us and we gotta get off this mountain. I'll be fine as soon as I get some coffee in me," McAuliff said. "I suppose Corcoran has the brandy with him?"

"I got some whiskey in my saddlebags." Amos White said. "We can use it to clean these wounds."

"We can clean the wounds with what's left over after I get my coffee cup full first," McAuliff chuckled. "You up to riding fairly hard through what's about to happen, Mr. White?"

"It's just tore up skin and meat from that busted up bullet. Soon as I get it cleaned up and bandaged, I'll be able to ride just fine. Hate to ride off and leave Corcoran, though."

"Neither one of us is up to gettin' in a fight in the middle of a blizzard, youngster. If we're gonna live, we gotta move out of here fast."

Amos White noticed for the first time how unsteady Sandy was, saw him have to brace himself standing up, weave around getting to his horse. *I can't let this man die up here. I'm not hurt half as bad as he is.* "Come on, Sandy, I got your back all the way down."

The wind, screeching down through the trees and rocks, was filled with blankets of snow that were piling up fast. "Won't be long, Amos, and we won't be seeing much. Let's tie the horses together. You ride your horse behind me, and I'll tie your horse off to my saddle horn. We don't want to get separated."

"No, Sandy. I'll lead. Old Rain in the Face is far stronger than that nag you've been left with."

Owens' horse was still limping but Sandy McAulif wasn't planning to make their run off the mountain a race, and they made their way back through the rocks and trees to the main trail without difficulty. The snow was drifting because of the high winds, visibility was down to yards, and the intense cold was beginning to take effect.

McAuliff was wrapped in a wool mountain man's Capote while White had a heavy bear skin coat on. The cold had one positive aspect though, it lessened the pain each was suffering. Or, maybe the pain of the cold was more than that of the wounds. They were hunched down in their saddles, feeling the pains of both, letting the horses pick their way down the single-track trail. They rode until it was simply too dark to see the trail under their saddles and moved off into a stand of pine trees. They fell into drifts that were such that the horses had to plunge and buck their way through, and they and their riders tired quickly.

Wind driven snow drifted deep, pine boughs broke free and sailed dangerously about, and trying to make a secure camp was going to be difficult at best. There were large rock formations and stands of trees, however, that could be to their benefit.

"Try to get some kind of lean-to up, Amos, and I'll work on getting a fire started." White leaned some long broken pine branches downwind and against a rock outcrop, added more in a criss-cross pattern, and had a bit of shelter for the two of them. They were out of the wind.

McAuliff, slow as molasses, gathered broken limbs and simply piled them up at the front of the lean-to. "Tired, Amos, and dizzy. Can't see very well." He put together a little mound of kindling-size pieces over a goodly pile of black powder, and struck his flint. "That's how you start a fire," he wanted to chuckle and couldn't. Tried to stand and couldn't. He was on his knees piling more wood on. Being behind the outcrop helped keep the gale force winds from scattering the fire and threw heat into their little den.

It was the stomach cramps, nausea, that slowed the old man down. His vision was failing from the blow to the head, he was dizzy just bending to strike the flint, he had to hold onto anything to keep from pitching forward. "I'm sick, Amos," he whispered.

Sandy McAuliff took a step into the lean-to and fell on his face in the snow and rocks. "Sandy," White yelled, rushing to the downed man. "Sandy, come on, old-timer, come on." He half carried, half dragged McAuliff all the way into the lean-to and laid him out on a bedroll and got him covered in wool blankets.

McAuliff moaned, jerked around a bit, and tried to sit up. "What happened?" The old man's head was spinning, he couldn't even sit up without feeling as if he would fall on his face again. He wretched, but there was nothing to come up. *We're not gonna make it this time. I can almost feel that secret door coming open. I'm not ready to die, got too much to live for, got this youngster with a badge to get off this mountain.* He could feel that he was losing consciousness again. "I'm sorry, General," he muttered.

"You passed out. You took one hell of a hit. I'll get coffee going and we'll have something to eat. We haven't eaten all day, old man. And, I ain't a general." The only food is what White had in his saddlebags since Owens stole McAuliff's horse. He kept the fire going hot, had coffee boiling in minutes and went through their stores. *Wonder why he called me general?*

"Not good," Amos White muttered. They were stretched out on their bedrolls looking out across the fire, watching the snow pile up. It was already almost a foot deep. "Maybe a pound of elk meat, a little bag of biscuits, and enough coffee for about four more pots. We got to get off this mountain tomorrow." As many buckaroos have learned to do, White woke up about every two hours during the night and kept that fire blazing. It seemed that each time, the storm was blowing and snowing even harder. He heard heavy, labored breathing from McAuliff

McAuliff talked nonsense all night long. Giving orders to other guides and trackers, responding to orders given by a general, making sure everyone understood how dangerous the situation was. "That blow to the head really jumbled things up in there," Amos muttered. "At least he was able to keep some of the food down. God, I love this old man and I ain't gonna let him die out here."

Corcoran was riding hard through blowing snow and almost felt the bullet passing over his head. He grabbed his rifle and jumped out of the saddle, racing for a downed tree off to the side of the trail, when another bullet blew bark and wood in front of him. *Bastard's come close twice now. That's all he gets.*

The wind was howling, the snow was thick, and it was icy cold. Corcoran felt warmed by the anger boiling inside. And the anxiety of knowing a huge storm was pounding the mountains. He wormed his way around the tree and tried to find Owens through the thick snow curtain.

"Come on, you train wreckin' bastard, show yourself." It wasn't sight, but rather sound, that gave Owens' position away. The outlaw's feet went out from under him on some icy rock and he tumbled about ten feet down the mountain. "Gotcha," Corcoran snickered.

Corcoran moved quickly forward, tucked in behind a rock, spotted Owens trying to get to his feet, and shot him. Owens was face down in the snow, trying to roll over, trying to reach his dropped handgun, moaning in pain. "Sure would like to kill your filthy body, but this old badge I wear just won't let me do that. Thought I killed ya. Damn shame I was such a poor shot."

He rolled Owens over, relieved him of his sidearm and his knife, and moved him down to the fallen tree. Owens wasn't half the threat the blizzard was, and Corcoran moved back up the side of the mountain, found Sandy's horse, and brought him down. He got snow moved from the lee side of a downed tree, gathered as much wood as he could and got a fire started. Owens was near the fire and Corcoran took the time to check his wound.

"I might just let you die and come back for your bones come spring, you bank robbin' bastard." He had the man's shirt open, saw where the bullet tore through, low on the shoulder, breaking bones and ripping flesh. There was extreme damage to the top of Owens' chest.

"Rifles do a good job stopping murdering bastards like you. I'm gonna splash a wee bit of brandy on that mess and wrap it up. If you die, remember this, it's your own fault.

"What brought you to Eureka, Owens? The bank isn't that well known outside these parts. Why did you and Dupree come here?"

"Dupree was in prison with a rustler and killer who told him about the bank and to find Colonel Cornell who already had a plan. Dupree believed him. Bastard kid at the bank lied to us is what went wrong." Owens was having a hard time talking, even breathing, but he heard Corcoran laugh right out at his last statement.

"Kid didn't lie, Owens. I set you up. Think that bullet ripped out some of your lung. You're gonna die because of a blow-hard lying colonel and one smart deputy sheriff."

Rafferty saw the fire and hollered out before riding to it. "You fixin' supper Corcoran? Comin' in."

"Bout time you got here. Sure, and just look. Had to capture this crazed bank robbin', train wrecking, bandito all by myself. Had to make up camp all by myself. And, now, here you are expecting to be served supper. Never think of anyone else, do you?"

"What a splendid effort, Mr. Corcoran. Let's not stay here, though, old man. We got to get off this mountain. There's gonna be three feet of snow and ten foot drifts before morning."

"I know," Corcoran said, quietly. "Glad you're here, Rafferty. Let's eat something and move out. He's hurt bad so we'll need to tie him off."

"Why not just let him die. Hell of lot easier to move a body."

"I know," Corcoran almost whispered. "I'm a man of principles, Sonny. It's the hardest part of being a lawman." Rafferty patted him on the shoulder, knew there wasn't anything to say, and tended the fire.

They soaked elk meat in boiling coffee, ate sourdough biscuits, and were in the saddle in fifteen minutes. The snow was driven by gale force winds and drifts were already forming. "Ride until we can't see the trail is best," Corcoran said and had to laugh. *Hell, can't see the trail now.* He led, leading Owens' horse, and having Rafferty's horse tied to Owens'. "Separated, we die, Sonny. We ride together all the way down."

It was the fallen trees blocking the trail that made things so hard. Off the trail, the horses would have to fight through deep drifts, plunging, bucking, driving forward, panting, and sweating in bitter cold. They wore out fast, the riders were desperately tired, and there was no end in sight.

How long could they go on like this? Corcoran and

Rafferty were in excellent physical condition and were being driven to exhaustion. How long would Corcoran's best friend, Sandy McAuliff be able to fight these insane forces of nature. On top of fallen trees and branches blocking the trails, there were rock slides to contend with. Loosely jumbled piles of rocks suddenly falling from the incredible weight of snow, letting loose tons of ice, snow, and rock, which could knock a horse down and bury its rider.

And, if it didn't, it meant the riders would have to ride around it, getting off the trail, fighting drifts and debris, falling or fallen trees, and unseen obstacles buried in the deep white fluff. Man and beast teamed against the incredible forces of nature, high on a mountain ridge, in the middle of nowhere, Nevada.

CHAPTER FIFTEEN

"Papa, you have to, and you know it. Those men will die. They are your friends, people you've known for years, on that mountain, in that blizzard. We have to." Hank Whipple hadn't seen his daughter this distraught since she was a little girl. It was worry, anger, and something else, he thought he saw. It was Amos White she was worrying over when she said, "those men," or "People you've known." When the massive early winter storm descended on the valley, Helen Whipple's first thoughts were on Amos White, high in the Cortez Range, searching for a killer. The older rancher saw it in her eyes.

"You've known Terrence Corcoran since he moved to Eureka County, Hank. You can't let that man die up there." Esmeralda Whipple stood at the kitchen stove, hands on her ample hips, giving her husband the what-for. Hank Whipple was still smarting from the stand off with Amos White, but knew his wife and daughter were right. "Put together your best buckaroos, Hank, and save those men."

"You mean save Amos, don't you?" There was the slightest hint of a grin when he asked his daughter. Esmeralda couldn't hold back the chuckle.

The biggest fight was about to happen as Hank Whipple had five of his men saddled, their saddlebags filled with food and other supplies. Helen Whipple rode out of the barn on her fine ranch gelding, covered in a buffalo coat and high boots. "Where do you think you're going, young lady?"

"I'm riding with you, Papa. Those are my friends, too. They're gonna need someone who knows how to stitch a wound, set a bone, and talk nice at a fire. I'm riding with you."

"Now, you listen, girl," Hank Whipple started to say, but was cut off mid sentence.

"No! You listen, Hank Whipple, Papa," she barked. "I'm a full grown woman who knows how to care for people. They need me up there. You need me on this ride." Her black eyes blazed, her fists were doubled up, and she sat, straight as a ram-rod in her saddle. "Time's a wastin'. I'm going," she said, touching her spurs and leading the men off.

Hank Whipple moved right up alongside his beautiful daughter and saw a defiant and brave woman riding into the jaws of a terrible storm. It was pride that beamed from his weathered face and a gentle smile offered across the couple of feet when she looked toward him.

"I don't say these kinds of things very often, Helen. It ain't in me, I guess, but I'm glad you're riding with us. You and your mother are my strength in life. I'd a probably just been a drifter, tramp buckaroo, if it weren't for your mother. Then, there you were, and looky now. Damn me but I'm one lucky man."

"I love you too, Papa," she murmured, turning her head so he wouldn't see the tears.

The ride from the Rocking W south to where the Arnold brothers had the cattle hidden took the rest of the day, and camp was made up at the canyon's mouth. The storm had the valley covered in several inches of snow by the time they got there. "That wind's gonna get fierce by the time we get started in the morning," Whipple said.

"The only thing we know for sure is, Corcoran and his posse are on that mountain right now, chasing a killer. We have food and blankets, a few extra horses, and medical supplies, and they're gonna need everything we have, if we're able to find them. We'll leave out at first light, and we'll be riding through some deep drifts."

Three of the five buckaroos riding with Whipple were leading extra horses, just in case, and the group led out, single file after filling up with coffee, side meat, and biscuits. Helen rode immediately behind her father who had one of the buckaroos leading, breaking trail.

"When you feel your horse tiring, drop back and someone else will lead. We ain't here to be killing no horses." The ride was uphill, following the ancient Indian trail deep into the Cortez Range. It wound around mountain shoulders, threaded through broken rock fields, and fought its way over high rocky passes. Snow was blown into their faces at hurricane force, drifts as high as eight feet closed their way and if they couldn't break through them they had to find a way around them. Some horses just quit, wouldn't fight any more, and were left to be picked up on the way down.

"My God, Papa, can those men still be alive? How did they survive the night?" Her words said "men," but her mind was fixated on just one man, Amos White. She remembered all those years growing up around the White Ranch. Amos was her first love, but she was ten and he was seventeen. That was why she kicked dirt on his new boots.

It was the only way I could get him to notice me. Him strutting around with shiny boots, talking about dancing with some girl, not me. She wanted to giggle, but where she was, what she was riding through, what they might find, filled her mind, and she shivered in fear instead. The storm had started the day before and they were still in low country. How deep were those drifts where Amos was? How high up this dreadful range was he? Would Amos White still be alive?

"Wake up, Sandy. Wake up," Amos White said, twice more, shaking the old tracker. The fire was blazing but couldn't fight off the bitter cold of the morning. McAuliff was alive, but White couldn't wake him up. He shook him harder, poked him, not too gently, in the ribs, and finally got a grunt from the old man. "Wake up, Sandy. We gotta get moving."

The blow to the head was more than a serious wound, the tracker knew it, and was weak and dizzy. "No balance, Amos. Sick to my stomach and no balance. Maybe it be best if you just ride on, save yourself."

"That ain't gonna happen, Sandy." *How can he think that I would ride off and leave him? No, old man, I ain't ridin' off and leavin' you. It's because of you that I'm here, a deputy sheriff.* "Let's get some coffee and a biscuit in you, get some water drank, and get you on your feet."

Amos White gave the impression that he did things like this every day of the week. He was far more afraid than any man would ever know. He got lost in these mountains once, when he was about eight years old and it was terrifying. *This isn't like that, but I'm just as terrified. I can't let this old man die, I'm not going to kill us both, either.*

"Come on, Sandy, let's get you on your feet. You'll feel better." It took all his strength to get the man standing. "That's the way, one foot at a time, Sandy. Come on, now," he urged, over and over.

There was no let up in the storm as the light of day fought its way in. It was a tempest outside their lean-to, with drifts covering everything. Amos fought his way through the snow to the horses and got them saddled. He walked them to the shelter and tied them off, slipped inside and found McAuliff still standing, but hanging on to one of the pine boughs.

"I'm dizzy as hell, Amos. You'll have to keep a close eye on me." He worked his way out of their hovel and with some help got in the saddle. He had to stop every couple of steps, wretch, try to catch his breath, and continue. "Slow and easy will get us off the mountain, Amos, but it will kill the horses. We'll be lucky to make eight miles today."

Amos White held back his scoff. McAuliff was

being optimistic with his eight miles talk, and White figured they'd be lucky to do two. He led them out and onto what he thought would be the trail. The old man might be sick as a dog but his mountain knowledge was still with him. "Use the trees and what rocks can be seen to keep you on the trail, Amos," Sandy said. "Don't try to look for the trail. It's deep down under its winter blanket right now. Your horse will probably do better than either one of us."

Amos White had a big, strong horse, but the storm was far stronger. It built drifts higher than the saddle he rode on, toppled trees a hundred feet long across the trail that he had to lead them around, and blew ice deep into McAuliff's Capote and his bear skin robe. They'd go forward five hundred yards and backtrack three hundred to get around an obstacle. After three hours, White estimated they may have made a mile and his horse needed time to blow.

McAuliff was riding a horse that started the journey with a limp, but following, not leading, was far easier on the animal and on Sandy. "Five minutes, Amos, that's all. Can't let these animals chill up, we'll never get 'em moving again. Five minutes, boy." Even the old tracker's voice had weakened and White felt a deep and penetrating fear of impending loss.

I've never been in this kind of situation, he thought,

feeling the sting of icy crystals hitting his face at more than sixty miles an hour. *That old man has helped me at every turn of my life since dad gave up the ranch. I ain't gonna let him die, and if we do have to, I'm gonna make his journey as easy as possible.*

Amos White knew there wasn't time nor did he have the ability to get a fire started, and he wanted coffee laced with some good whiskey in the worst way. "Here, Sandy, take a quick sip of whiskey and we'll get started again. Old Rain in the Face is a good horse, but this is the hardest work he's ever had to do."

"Lost half a troop in a storm like this," McAuliff all but whispered. He had a headache, sick stomach, and felt as if he would fall from the saddle at any moment, but still had a story to tell. He took a long sip of whiskey, coughed, and let his eyes roam through the blizzard. "We'll be crossing a ridge shortly, Amos, and the wind will be like a cyclone. Don't lose me, I won't lose you."

Amos took the bottle back and tucked it inside his coat, nudging his horse back into the struggle. "We'll find a place to hole up on the other side of the ridge, Sandy. We need to get some food in you. Yell out if you can't hang on."

Crossing the ridge was far worse than McAuliff had described. Incredible winds lashed the horses and riders, the ground in places didn't have a single snowflake but just feet away would be a drift ten deep. Amos White had to step out of the saddle and try to lead the horses. The wind all but tore him lose twice, and that would probably have led to both their deaths. The horses had their heads as low as they could, almost scraping their noses on rocks and ice. McAuliff was bent double in his saddle, hanging on to the saddle horn to keep from being blown right off his mount.

"I have to walk, Sandy. Too dangerous to try and stay in the saddle." He fashioned a rope harness around McAuliff to keep him in the saddle and fought his way through the ferocious storm, leading the two horses. Footing was terrible, the snow was knee high in places and much deeper in other places. Ice made for unsure footing for man and horses. Two feet, five feet, how long before there were no more feet forward?

Amos White turned to look back at McAuliff as often as he dared, scared witless that he'd find a riderless horse. It seemed like hours to get across the ridge and on the trail leading down the other side, but they made it, and White, remounted, pulled them to a stop under a tall pine tree, not really out of the wind, but a little bit, anyway.

"Sandy," White called out, as the man swayed in the saddle, almost falling. Amos grabbed him and

McAuliff jerked awake. "Stay with me, Sandy. We'll take a short break and find a camp for the night. It's almost dark." He passed a canteen to the old tracker. "Drink some of this if it's not frozen." They both tried to chuckle through their icy lips, face, and hair, and couldn't.

Amos led them slowly through deep snow to a stand of trees and another rock outcrop, got McAuliff off his horse and settled next to a rock and out of the wind. Horses were tended to as much as could be done, a haphazard lean-to was built, and a huge fire was lit. hurricane winds had blown tree limbs, entire trees down, and it was easier to just drag a huge limb onto the fire. "Gotta get you warm and fed, Sandy. Gotta." *We're ten miles or more from that rustler's canyon and we have enough food for one day. We can't make ten miles in one day. In this storm we'll be lucky to make ten miles in three days. How am I gonna keep that man alive?*

Corcoran broke trail for the first hour then let Sonny Rafferty take the lead. They traded off through hours of incredible cold and wind. Everything mother nature could throw at them they fought through, and it was mid-day that Corcoran saw Oscar Owens slumped in the saddle and almost blue.

"He's gone, Sonny. Let's take a short break for the

horses to blow and tie him across the saddle. Just a few minutes, though."

"Lost a good horse letting him stand too long after a really hard ride. We haven't made much for distance."

"A few miles. Going back and forth like this, breaking trail, makes it better for us and the horses. I'm worried about old Sandy McAuliff, though. The way you described it, it must have been a hell of a crack to the head. He's a tiger, though. Problem is, we have his food. All they have is what Amos White had in his saddlebags. We gotta catch them."

"I doubt they're moving fast," Rafferty chuckled. Let's have another drink of that brandy, old man. Why did I let you talk me into coming along on this little hike?"

"It was your idea when you shot at me. You and lettin' your cows just wander off."

They fought their way through the maelstrom until it got too dark to go any further and found a spot somewhat out of the wind to camp. They dug out an area behind a big stand of rocks, built a fire out from the rocks, and laid their bedrolls between the fire and rocks. It took a little extra black powder to get the fire started but it was hot soon. They had coffee and brandy, elk meat, and sourdough biscuits for supper.

"Just like downtown, eh?" Corcoran laughed.

"Room service with a smile. We're gonna die tomorrow if we don't make more progress than today."

"I always wanted to ride with a quitter," Rafferty laughed. "Ain't no storm big enough to take out the both of us at the same time."

"Yup," is all Corcoran chuckled, rolling over in his blankets. "Keep that fire hot, Sonny, and I'd like pancakes for breakfast."

"They'll be hot and covered in syrup, Mr. Corcoran, sir." Rafferty was still laughing as he built the fire up. *What the hell am I doing up here, riding with Terrence? Sure, he's a badge wearin' lawman, but I'm not. I got no business being here at all, getting shot at, fighting my way through a terrible storm. I should be back at the Raines ranch watching the cows. What drives a man like Corcoran to think it's his duty to chase a mad man into these mountains in a blizzard?*

Well, hell, Sonny, it's the same thing that drives you to find the men who stole your cattle. And now I'm helping to bring the dead body of a man who had nothing to do with my cattle, the brand I work for, or even the territory I live in. I'm here because I'm Corcoran's friend and he needed a friend.

Both men were up before sunrise, hot coffee and sidemeat, sourdough biscuits softened in the coffee in their bellies, and saddles on their horses. "One more night is all we have to make, I think," Corcoran said. The wind was cyclonic, the snow epic, and the ride dangerous for horse and man. They found numerous trees blocking the trail, great drifts reaching ten feet and more deep they couldn't plow through, over, or around, and as the day slowly came to an end, indications that there were others on the trail.

Irregular mounds in the drifts, a pile of road apples was the giveaway. "I sure hope that's Amos and Sandy," Corcoran muttered. "Your horse is about done in, Sonny. We gotta hole up and soon."

"He twisted that leg bad when those rocks let loose on us. He needs a good night. I think I'll ride McAuliff's horse tomorrow and let the dead man ride this one."

"We may just give the dead man a decent burial and pony your horse the rest of the way. We got a long way to go to get off this mountain. We ain't anywhere near safe."

"If what we're looking at are McAuliff's tracks, we'll catch up with them tomorrow, Corcoran. Let's make another mile and find some trees to burn."

"It's been a real pleasure going on this little camping trip with you, Sonny. We might think about doing this more often." There was hearty laughter from two bone-weary men high in the Nevada wilderness.

CHAPTER SIXTEEN

"Cold," she said, pulling a wool blanket around her shoulders. The fire was warm but the wind wasn't, and the snow was deep. "I've never been high in the mountains in the winter, Papa. Is it always like this?"

"Worst storm I've ever been in," Hank Whipple said. "We're lucky, though, girl. We have fresh horses, had good hot food this morning, and those poor devils up there got nothing." He motioned for his crew to move out and he led the way with Helen following. The trail was already fully covered and Whipple called another rider up front after about an hour.

Helen was quiet as they rode, took in all the sights and sounds of the storm's fury and had terrible visions of what they might find. Would Amos White survive this incredible show of nature? He was so big and strong, but this wind, this freezing cold, was he that big? She wanted to put the spurs to that beast she was riding and fought to control her emotions. *I could spend the rest of my life with that monster of a man. We have to save them.*

"How far do we have to go?" She asked her father riding in front of her.

"Until we find them," he answered. "We'll ride until dark, camp out, and ride till dark tomorrow. Storms like this one usually break after the second day. I hope this one does."

Getting around the downed trees was the hardest, Helen thought, but they also encountered one rock fall that almost got the lead man. From time to time, there would be a break in the wind and the snow would fall almost straight down, great huge flakes, softly falling onto deep drifts. "It's beautiful," she said once and her father just scowled.

She's right though. He took that moment to look around them, at trees drooping dangerously with their load of white stuff. *If I could sit behind a window, near a hot fireplace and look at all this, I too would call it beautiful. Tomorrow, when the sun comes out, when the wind is used up and there's no more snow in the heavens, it will be beautiful.* Whipple looked at his daughter, sitting straight in the saddle, determined to save her man, and his heart felt like it would break. *We must find those men alive.*

The first day ended without Whipple's party finding Corcoran and the posse, and at camp the following morning there was discussion about turning back. "We're following a trail we know those men left on, but we don't know they stayed on it. We're putting ourselves in the kind of danger we think we're saving them from," one of the cowhands growled.

A couple of the men standing around the fire seemed to agree. "No, Buster, we ain't turning back." Hank Whipple had a tin cup half filled with coffee and the other half good brandy. "First off, they captured the rustlers and returned our cattle. Second, Corcoran's the best friend a rancher has in the Diamond Valley, and he needs help. Along with that, a Raines' buckaroo is riding with Corcoran, and Amos White is in the posse, wearing a badge. Those are our neighbors, our friends, looking at a cold hard death on this mountain. We will ride." Nobody argued with the big man and horses and gear were made ready.

Helen grabbed the big tough rancher and wrapped her arms around him, blubbering like a baby. "You're the best man in the whole world, Papa."

The higher they rode the harder it became. Drifts were incredible, trees were down everywhere, and forward progress was slow. "We're about five miles or so from the crest, Boss," the lead man hollered back.

"Doubt if we'll make it before dark."

"It's a hell of a thing to say, Helen," Hank Whipple said, riding alongside his daughter. "With all this snow this early in the season, we'll have good grass all next summer. Let's find those boys and celebrate that fact."

She had to laugh despite the fear that gripped her heart. *What good is all the good grass in the world if I can't have the man I want? The terrible part is, he's right, damn it. I want good grass and Amos White. That's why I'm here.*

Amos had dropped back to ride alongside Sandy McAuliff. The old tracker had weakened considerably overnight, couldn't keep even a biscuit and coffee down, and seemed to want to talk incessantly. "We'll keep riding until we find sunshine, Sandy," Amos White said. They were moving slowly through deep snow, gale force winds driving tons of snow hampered their vision and their way.

Sandy was incoherent most of the time, but talking. Some of the time he appeared to be telling stories of his younger days, some of the time having conversations with someone, often called general. And some of the time just making noises that might have started out being words. Amos White had never been with an older man in these dire straits. Didn't know if he was doing the right thing or was slowly killing his friend.

This is how I'm checking out, trying to keep an old man I love, as much as if he were my father, alive. He sat bolt upright in the saddle and squared his shoulders. *No! I'm not checking out and neither is old Sandy. This is not the end of the world, damn it.*

As if in a delirious dream, Sandy McAuliff told stories of his days tracking and guiding for the army as civilization moved slowly from the great plains into the majestic Rocky Mountains. He told of Indian battles, inept officers, gallant fighting on both sides. He had a high fever, hadn't been able to keep food down since that terrible bash to the head, and was only alive through sheer will.

White was trying to figure out how far they might be from that canyon used by the Arnold brothers. "We'll be away from the brute force of this storm if we can make that cut off canyon, Sandy. Can't be too far in front of us." He found himself talking to McAuliff even though the old man didn't seem able to hear him. McAuliff was talking as well, but not about anything Amos could relate to.

"Shush, Sandy," Amos said, pulling the two horses to a stop. "Listen. Be quiet now and listen." He was sure he heard a voice, a man's voice, not calling out, just talking. "Maybe I'm losing my mind, too," he said. He turned in the saddle to look behind them before getting back underway and saw what was surely a man on horseback, despite the heavy coat of blowing snow.

"Hello, the rider," he yelled into the storm's wrath, and watched the horseman sit straight up in the saddle. All at once there was a second rider and the two were plunging toward him, rearing and plunging through the snow, and for sure, toward him.

"Corcoran," White howled. "It's really you. Oh, God, I'm glad to see you. Sandy's in trouble."

It was a grand, if short, celebration, men hugging men, men whopping men across the shoulders, men worried that one of them was in his last hours. "Let's find some rocks to get behind and get a fire started," Corcoran said. "I've seen this before and it ain't pretty. He needs to be warm, under blankets, and in front of a fire. He needs to sleep warm for a long time."

With two helpers, Amos White had a substantial lean-to put together along the side of an outcropping and out of the wind. There was no shortage of downed wood. Logs, small trees actually, were brought in, and a bonfire was lit. "Let the old gentleman sleep the rest of today and tonight and we'll build a travois for the rest of his journey." Corcoran carried McAuliff into the lean-to and wrapped him in wool blankets. "Every time he wakes, feed him something. Good meat, strong coffee, a taste of whiskey, something. He's lost the will to live and food will help bring him back."

"He hasn't kept anything down for two days, Corcoran. Soft biscuits, even. I'm not gonna let him die like this."

"No, you're not, and neither am I. Get him so warm he wants to throw that buffalo robe away and then try to feed him," Corcoran laughed.

Amos White didn't want to bring it up but finally felt it had to be asked. "You weren't able to catch up to Owens?"

"Corcoran got him good," Sonny Rafferty said. "Fool died on the trek back." He hunched down near the fire and gave Amos White a long look. "You weren't always this big, Amos. I remember you as a boy on your father's ranch. Your father was a good man, just wasn't much of a rancher. You gonna stay with the badge?"

"I think this is my fourth, or maybe fifth, day wearin' one," he joshed. "Pa gave up the ranch and lives in Winnemucca now, working at the stockyards. Loves it, he says. You been with the Raines family for a long time."

"Best brand I've ever rode for, boy. You stick with Corcoran and you'll either be a good lawman or suffer an early death. I've known that man for a long time and he doesn't know the meaning of the word fear.

You did a good job keeping McAuliff alive. We ain't out of this yet, though."

The storm ended abruptly sometime late that night. The wind let up, the snow quit falling, and the temperature dove into negative numbers. Numbing, bone-chilling cold greeted the four men along with a bright sun shining through scattered clouds. "This will make it a little easier but those snow drifts will still be there, boys," Rafferty laughed. He had the last watch, keeping the fire blazing. "Coffee's hot."

"Should make rustler's canyon before dark. Let's eat well, get Sandy loaded on that travois, and make tracks," Corcoran said. "We need to be off this mountain by tonight. The sun will melt the surface of the snow, then freeze it bad tonight. We'd be breaking ice tomorrow and that kills horses."

"Sandy's having a hard time breathing, Corcoran," Amos White said. "He wants to see you. He did eat a little bit and keep it down."

Corcoran slipped into the lean-to and found Sandy McAuliff half sitting up. "Morning, old man. You're looking a little better than last time I saw you."

"I'm not gonna make it, Corcoran. Don't try to be nice. Feel the back of my head where that rifle cracked me. My skull is broke. I can feel where the bone's are all busted up."

His eyes were clear and his voice had strength to it, a far cry from the night before. Corcoran looked at the bowl on the side of the bedroll and saw that it was empty and smiled at his long-time friend. "Nope, old man, that ain't the case. Your old skin is all wrinkled up, caked with frozen blood and hair, but you ain't feeling broken skull bones. Sides that, you ate all your food, drank your coffee, and had a shot of brandy, too. Nope, you ain't gonna die today."

"Well, there's somethin' I gotta tell you just in case I do. Back twenty years or more, me and a couple of friends found a steel strong box hidden in a cave. It was filled with gold coins, hundreds of them. There weren't no name on the box, nothing but gold inside, and we split them twenty dollar coins up between us.Weren't against the law," he snapped, not letting Corcoran say anything. Corcoran just smiled and settled down on his haunches. "We each took two hundred of those double eagles, and the good thing was, we each had a pack mule to carry all that gold. Well, me and another one left out for a city and run smack into a bunch of angry Sioux. Fought them off for two days, lost my friend, but them Indians gave it up and left off.

"Now, I had two pack mules, two saddle horses, and four hundred double eagles all to myself. Still got most of 'em, Corcoran." He was able to give off a cackle of a laugh. "When I die, I want you to have them. There's a hole in the floor under my bed, and a tin box is buried in that hole, filled with gold. It's yours, boy."

"It ain't mine 'till you die, Sandy, and you ain't dyin' on this trip. Maybe next time, but you ain't dyin' this time." Corcoran got up quickly and stepped out of the lean-to before Sandy could see the tears in his eyes.

"Damn old fool, tellin' me that," he muttered. He walked behind a tree and stood tall and quiet. "Why'd he have to go and do that. Why couldn't he just have wrote it down somewhere." He remembered the ride they made after the Humboldt Charley gang, about the elk hunts the two made into the Diamond Mountains, and the many long nights of storytelling around campfires.

"Old coot's too tough to die, anyway," he finally said and walked back to the fire. "Let's get this army on the road. Day's half gone, now. Move it." A close look at the dirty face would reveal the tracks of the tears.

"Do you think one of us should ride ahead and try to find help?" Amos White wanted to get help for McAuliff as quickly as possible.

"Don't think anyone of us would be able to ride much faster than we are right now, Amos," Corcoran said. "All we'd do is kill us a horse. No, we aren't out of danger yet and it's best if we stick together. You take point and bust us a good trail for that travois."

CHAPTER SEVENTEEN

"You were right, Papa. It's a beautiful morning. No wind." The cold was not driven by high winds and the sun's warmth spread through her wool blanket, tightly wrapped about her shoulders. "Will we find them today?"

"If we don't, I'm afraid we will have to turn back. We'll be getting so high in these mountains that the drifts will be deeper than the horses are tall. With clear skies and no wind, we'll have good visibility."

Looking out across what appeared to be a vast plain or high plateau, Helen was aware that what she thought she was seeing was flat, level ground. It was actually very hilly, but the valleys between the hills were filled with wind-drifted snow. I would be impossible to ride out across that. A few points of steep ground were barren of snow while it might be twenty feet deep on the other side.

"I don't believe Amos would quit, Papa. Let's not think about quitting. I won't quit," she said. Her eyes showed just how frightened the young girl was and Hank Whipple slipped his arm around her and held her tight.

"We'll work hard to find them," He said.

Helen took the first lead, letting her strong horse move through the heavy snow. It was getting around all the blown down debris that made things so difficult. After an hour or so, she gave up the lead to her father. After that, one after another, each of the five buckaroos took the lead.

"Look," Hank Whipple called out early that afternoon. The bunch of them were exhausted, their horses covered in perspiration, everyone wanting to take a break. "Is that movement?" He was pointing toward a stand of pines about a mile up the side of the mountain. "I can't tell if those are horses or deer, but something's moving down that hillside."

The group stayed in place, everyone straining to tell what it was moving down the mountain. Bright sun splashed across blinding fresh snow made for poor vision. "Them's horses, Hank," one of the buckaroos said. "Five horses and one of 'em's pulling something."

Helen's heart was pounding furiously and she took

the lead, trying to get to those men too fast. "Slow it down, girl," Hank Whipple called out. "Ain't no good killin' a horse. We'll get to them." He watched her slow back to a good walk and looked around where they were.

"Pete, I want you and the boys to ride over to where those rocks and trees are. Build us a good camp. At least two or three lean-tos, good fire pits, and cleared of snow and ice. Make it safe from the winds that are sure to return. Helen, you and I will ride to Corcoran and bring them in. No rushing, get the job done right."

The buckaroos had been through the drill more than once, caught in the high country by rogue storms while tending the herd, and got right on it. Hank Whipple took the lead and he and Helen started back up the trail.

Helen wanted to break free, rush headlong, and fought if off. "They stopped when they spotted us, Helen. It won't be long and we can lead them to a hot fire."

"You see that down there?" Corcoran and Rafferty were riding together and Amos White was leading the travois with McAuliff. "We got company coming, girls, let's get all prettied up. Can't tell who, but there's a swarm of 'em down there."

"I wonder why?" Sonny Rafferty said, quietly. "Who knows we're even up here? Sure wouldn't be a hunting party, though. We might want to make sure our guns aren't frozen." He pulled his revolver from its holster and tucked it inside his heavy coat, up against his body. Corcoran did the same.

"Might be a Shoshone hunting party, but that's damn doubtful," Corcoran said. "Nobody knows we're up here, as far as I know, so they ain't lookin' for us. I can't imagine why anyone would be on this mountain."

They continued moving down the trail, watching several of the group break off for a stand of pine trees, and two riders came on up the trail. "They're setting up to ambush us, Rafferty? Sure setting up to do something. What the hell are they doing out in a storm like this?"

"That's Hank Whipple and his daughter," Amos yelled out as the group got closer. "Helen knew I was riding up to find you, Corcoran. Must have convinced her father to organize a rescue when we didn't return. Happy days!"

The hour and half it took for the two groups to meet seemed like days to Helen, and when they did, she rushed to Amos's side. "You're okay," she smiled. "I was worried sick when you didn't come back down the mountain and made father come looking for you.

Oh, God, Amos, I was so worried. Don't ever do this to me again. No matter how long we're together."She realized what she'd said, turned bright red, but continued anyway. "When you shot Jonas Holiday because he struck me, I knew I loved you."

Amos found it hard to talk, his beard frozen, his heart thumping, and this gorgeous creature telling him she loved him. He smiled as best he could, and stammered something, finally saying something about getting down off the mountain.

"I got my boys setting up a good camp, Corcoran," Whipple said. "Glad you're along too, Rafferty. Get that killer, did you, Corcoran?"

"Got him dead, Hank. Amos White told us about him having to take your foreman out. Hope you're alright with that." Corcoran and Whipple went back years and there had never been trouble between the two. This wasn't the time or place for trouble to start.

"Had it coming, he did. Smacked my Helen. It should have been me taking him out. Glad you caught those rustlers, but you should have let us hang them."

"Pretty much what I told him, Hank," Rafferty laughed. "He told me to keep better watch of my cows."

Whipple tried his best not to chuckle, but couldn't. "You can be a real bastard sometimes, Corcoran. A real bastard. Let's get this mess down to that camp.

Your man needs doctoring and Helen is good at that."

Following the trail broken by Hank and his daughter made the ride down to the trees and rocks a lot easier and faster, and they found two big fires burning hot when they got there. "We brought plenty of fresh meat, even a couple of pies," Whipple said. They took care of their horses, then turned their attention to Sandy McAuliff.

"That was a most pleasant journey, Mr. White," McAuliff said when Amos got him free of the travois. The old tracker had color in his cheeks and a smile on his face. "Most pleasant." White helped him over to a spot set up for him next to a fire and Helen sat down next to him. "My head's all busted up, Helen Whipple, I'm not seeing well, and I hurt."

"That's why I'm here, Mr. McAuliff. I'm gonna stop the hurtin'."

"Call me Sandy. I always like it when pretty girls call me Sandy."

"Sounds to me like you're already half recovered, McAuliff," Corcoran laughed. "Watch him, Helen, he's a sneaky devil and he'll trick you for sure."

Corcoran motioned for Hank Whipple, Sonny Rafferty, and Amos White to join him at the other fire. "We're still in a mess, boys. Is anyone else hurt and not saying anything?" He looked about the group, letting his eyes fall on White. "Amos, Sonny told me you were shot, and you haven't said a word. Where?"

"When Owens jumped us, he fired a shot at me that hit a rock first. The mangled up bullet hit my leg. It's so cold, I haven't even felt it. I'm fine."

"That's how people lose legs, Amos." Hank Whipple said. "Ignoring a wound. Take care of it now. Go over to Helen, and she'll doctor you up. She's got all the stuff." Amos shook his head as if to pass it off, but a scowl from Corcoran got him moving toward Helen Whipple's fire pit.

"Anybody else?" Corcoran got shakes of heads and stirred the fire. "If McAuliff and Amos are up to it, then, let's plan on moving out in the morning. Breaking through your trail, Hank, should make it fairly easy. Can we bunk up at your place before we head back to Eureka?"

"It'll be a good two days to the Rocking W, and sure, you'll be more than welcome to stay with us as long as you need to."

"What Sandy needs more than anything else is rest. He's got some severe swelling where that rifle slammed into the back of his head. It should have killed him," Helen said. "He's hungry and thirsty, and that's a good sign. Help me get him laid out in one of those lean-tos and wrapped in wool blankets, and he'll be fine."

Amos picked McAuliff up like he was a foundling calf and carried him to a lean-to. "I got nicked by a stray bullet, Helen. Corcoran thinks you should take a look. Hurt when it happened, but no pain right now."

"You got shot? Oh, no, Amos. No," she cried. "Oh, let's get back to the fire. Show me. No, Amos." *Oh, Amos. I'll take care of you. So brave riding off to help Corcoran and getting shot. I'll take care of you.*

"It's all right, Helen. Just a nick. Pour some whiskey on it and it'll be fine." *Why do women get all upset like this over something as simple as a scratch? What would she do if it was a real wound, for heaven's sake?*

She gushed some more over the severity of the wound and Amos told her over again that it was just a scratch. "No, it isn't, Amos White," she said. "Look, see this bright red? That, my friend, is infection and if you had let it go another day, it would be gangrene. You would lose your leg. It's not just a scratch."

She showed her anger and her knowledge of wounds and Amos knew better than to argue with the lady. "That bullet was dirty, you wrapped it in a dirty rag, and didn't clean it properly, Amos. There's pieces of that rag stuck," she said, ripping a piece off. He could not control the yelp, and she chuckled. "If you didn't like that you won't like this, either."

He did his best not to howl when she wanted to clean the infected wound with the whiskey he suggested, but he let it out like a wolf at the full moon when she poured it on. "Oh, come now, Amos White, it's just a little scratch, isn't it?" She teased him. He thought about a lot of words he wanted to say and knew he wouldn't, and just sat scowling like a little boy.

"We'll do this again in the morning before we ride out, Amos. I'll take care of you. Don't plan on marrying a man with just one leg."

He still had a big dumb grin on his face when Sonny Rafferty sat down on a log next to him. "Looks like you got her throwed and tied. She's a keeper, Amos. You might be giving up that badge and running a big old cattle ranch sooner than you thought."

"She's so pretty," he said. *Give up the badge? Run a ranch? She said she wanted to marry me? I'm confused. Maybe I got a fever.*

Helen did all her doctoring in the morning, McAuliff was tied to the travois, Whipple's five buckaroos did the trail breaking, and the group moved out a little later than sunrise. "We have to do this with all the tradition that's called for, Amos," Helen said. They were riding side by side behind McAuliff's trundle. "You must ask Papa for my hand. Oh, Mama will be thrilled. She thinks you're the most handsome man in the world, next to Papa." She laughed and blushed at the same time.

Things were happening faster than Amos could think and despite his trying, he could not stop grinning. "I will, Helen. You know, I'm a deputy sheriff, and, well, I've got obligations."

"Of course you do. But you don't really want to be a deputy all your life, do you?"

He remembered conversations with Corcoran when he was approached for the job and in particular the big question Corcoran asked about him being married. When he said no, Corcoran said good. And now she's asking if he wants to be a deputy all his life. *That's the point isn't it? Can one be married and be a lawman? It's a dangerous job, I guess what we're doing right now proves that, so is it fair to a woman to ask her to be married to a lawman?*

"I would be terrified every day that you wouldn't be coming home or that you'd come home all broken up and shot to pieces. Talk to Papa, Amos. I want to be your wife and I want you to be home, safe, with me."

Safe? He thought about that, remembering the days on the old ranch. What was safe? He wondered. Was it riding with Corcoran through blizzards chasing a killer? Was it riding after rogue bulls high in Nevada's rugged mountains? "Do I want to be safe? I want to be with this wonderful girl," he murmured, "but what did she mean by safe?"

Amos knew he needed to talk to someone, but thought the best person would be Sandy McAuliff. After all, it was McAuliff who thought he would be a good deputy, and this trip had proved that he was a good deputy. He also remembered, vividly, what Sonny Rafferty said about running a big cattle ranch. Marrying the ranchers' daughter was not a bad idea. And when that daughter was the beautiful Helen Whipple, it was an excellent idea.

"I will, Helen. First chance I get. I want you to be my wife." *My God, what have I done?*

The day's ride put them at the rustlers' cut off canyon and a good warm camp. Snow on the valley floor had settled down, some had melted in the hot sun. There was a difference measured in thousands of feet altitude from where they were to where they had been. There were a few lingering drifts here and there. "A good hot supper and night's rest, and we'll be at the ranch sometime tomorrow," Hank Whipple said.

"A few thousand feet make a world of difference," Corcoran snorted. In the bright sun they could look up at the towering ridges, standing bright in the clear sky. "Looks almost serene from down here."

Helen spent an hour with Sandy McAuliff, seeing

to it that the wound on his head was mending properly, and talking about Amos White. "There's no infection, Sandy, and those stitches that you howled about are holding fine," she chuckled. "You and Amos are long time friends, aren't you?"

"His father wasn't much of a rancher, cattleman, I'm afraid, but that boy is. He worked in the mines for a short time when his father lost the ranch, and tried store keeping, but hated being trapped indoors all day. I aimed him at Corcoran and he took to that badge right away. If I had ever married, I'd want a son like Amos. He's good with horses, cattle, and now, outlaws," the old trapper cackled.

"I want him to be my husband and be a rancher, Sandy."

"Then tell him so, young lady. He sure does have his eyes on you. Tell him what you want. No reason to beat about the bushes when the rabbit's in plain sight." That brought a tinkle of laughter from her.

She didn't tell him they had talked about it. Just nodded and smiled. "Better have your supper and another good night's sleep. We'll clean that wound again in the morning." She went off to find her father and Sandy went to the cook fire. He was moving around with no help now that he was eating good.

"Big pot of beef stew, Sandy. Will you join me

for supper? Got two nice logs for us to sit on," Amos White said. "Something I want to bend your ear with." They had bowls of Rocking W beef stew, steaming in the icy air, and settled near the fire. "I want to marry that girl but she don't want me to be a lawman. Wants me to be safe, whatever that is."

"Everybody wants to be safe, boy, but sometimes things get in the way. What she wants is you runnin' the big cattle ranch. Old Hank and Esmeralda were only able to have one child, and the way I figure it, Hank is lookin' to back out of being a full-time rancher. He probably don't much care for turning it over to a teenage girl to run. Betcha money she knows that, too."

"I haven't been a lawman long enough to know what being a lawman is," Amos chuckled. "I surely do know something about buckarooin'. Papa wasn't a good rancher, wouldn't listen to those that were, but I listened and learned, saw his mistakes. Do you think I should talk to Hank? He's already upset that I shot his foreman."

"Which means, young man, that he needs a new foreman." McAuliff chuckled some and ate his bowl of stew watching Amos White fidget through his. White finally put his bowl down and looked around for Hank Whipple.

"Now or never, I guess."

CHAPTER EIGHTEEN

It was a slow ride into the Rocking W the next day. McAuliff on his travois, Helen and Amos riding side by side, and Corcoran having one argument after another with Rafferty. Hank Whipple sent his buckaroos on ahead to alert Esmeralda there would be guests. It was a pleasant day, not a cloud in sight, no wind, and lots of mud. They took a break for noon meal and Helen sat down with Amos.

"I know you talked to Papa, but you haven't said anything. Neither has he," Helen said.

"We had a very nice conversation, my dear lady. Your father gets right to the point, doesn't he. I wasn't very good at what I was supposed to be doing and he spent some time laughing at me. I guess he was getting even for me shooting Jonas Holiday. I finally just blurted out that I was in love with you and wanted his permission to ask you to marry me."

"Well? What was his answer. Come on, Amos, quit stalling," she said. She had her father's temper, or maybe it was her mother's, and he had to chuckle. "Don't be this way," she said and poked him in the shoulder.

Amos White took a deep breath and talked as fast as a Gatling gun rattled. "He said he'd rather his son-in-law be a rancher. I said I was. He said I should ask you to marry me. I said I would. He said, then you'll need a job other than deputy sheriff, and would I take the job of ranch foreman since I almost killed his current foreman."

She flung her arms around him and kissed him, then sat back, blushing. "Guess I shouldn't have done that," she said. He smiled and took her in his arms and kissed her back, over and over. After their quick meal, the troop was back on the trail and Corcoran motioned Amos up front with him.

"Looks like we need to talk some, Amos. You about to give up your long-time career as a lawman? Deputies don't usually go around kissing young girls or cow-towing with their fathers over an evening's campfire." He went out of his way not to smile or chuckle, which was difficult.

"Yup, we do need to talk, and I ain't very good at talking."

"Must have said something right to get kisses and hugs like that," he chuckled.

White blushed, lowered his eyes, coughed some, and slowly came to sit straight up, looking eye to eye with Corcoran. "I asked Hank Whipple if I could marry Helen and he said yes but only if I took the job of ranch foreman at the Rocking W. Please don't be angry with me, Sheriff. I was sincere when I took this job you offered. All of this stuff just happened."

"Stuff happens, Amos. That's what life is all about. You gotta help me get Sandy back home safe, get your reports written for the judge, and find me your replacement. When that's all done you can retire your badge, but not a minute sooner. I'm gonna miss you, boy. You stood up just like Sandy McAuliff said you would."

Amos stammered his thank you, shook hands with Corcoran. "Is being a lawman why you ain't married?"

"Back a few years, Amos, I was almost in the same position you are now," Corcoran said. Memories he thought he had safely tucked away in a cast iron safe, memories of the Lady with the Shaggy Hair smashed him across the side of the head. He spent the next ten minutes telling Amos White the sad story of how he lost the only woman he had ever truly loved.

"Yes, my young friend, I came that close to giving up the badge. It takes a very strong woman, one like Helen

Whipple to draw a man from this life. You will be a fine husband and father and run an upstanding ranch."

Amos forced tears back at Corcoran's story and slowly eased his horse back so he could talk with Hank Whipple. It was a long and easy ride the rest of the day. "I want to add a horse breeding program to our ranch and expand the herd some, Amos. You finish up your obligations to Corcoran and get back to our ranch, son," he almost smiled. *That's the kind of man I want running my ranch. He understands responsibility and obligations. I won't tell him but I'm glad he shot Jonas Holiday.*

The week at Whipple's ranch was a pleasant change from the ordeal on Cortez Mountain and with two women spending a great deal of time making him comfortable, Sandy McAuliff regained his strength quickly. "We'll be heading back to Eureka tomorrow morning, Hank. It's been a real pleasure enjoying your hospitality."

"You're welcome here anytime, Corcoran. Anytime. You've had quite a ride, captured the rustlers, killed the train robber, and saved your friend's life. Not bad, Corcoran. Not bad."

"And lost a fine deputy, you old codger," Corcoran laughed. "Might need your testimony at Arnold's trial, but that will be sometime down the line. They'll hold him in the Palisade jail, but the trial will be in Eureka, the county seat."

"Sure do want to see that man hang. Is that tin can of a jail safe? Hasn't never held nothing but a few drunks."

"It's got steel bars and rock walls, Hank. Arnold will stand trial and with many dead men to be responsible for, you'll probably get that wish to see him hanging."

"He sold off quite of bit of the rustled stock. I only got back some of what was stolen. It's hard enough to raise good beef without having to put up with the likes of Silas Arnold and his dim-witted brother."

Sonny Rafferty left off north for the Raines ranch and Corcoran led his group south toward Eureka at first light. "Now, you keep track of those critters, Rafferty. Don't be lettin' these snot nose criminals be stealin' 'em anymore."

"I'll do what I can, Corcoran, but it would help if we had decent law enforcement in this county. So long, Pard," he laughed, riding off in a mixed cloud of mud and dust, yahooing the whole way. Corcoran chuckled, then laughed right out, getting the troop under way.

"You gonna be okay to ride, Sandy? We could borrow a buggy from Whipple if you'd be more comfortable."

"Don't you even think that way, Terrence. I might be bit older than you, but I'm still tougher, and don't forget it."

Corcoran wondered if maybe the man might be at least as tough as he was. *Wonder what I'll be like when I'm an old beat up lawman? He be tellin' stories at every chance about what it was in his day. Hell, Terrence Corcoran, you'll sure have a few stories to tell.* He was riding with a grand smile, even a chuckle or two, listening to yet another fearsome story of winters in the Rocky Mountains and the plains.

Amos White didn't take part in the lively conversations, he was too busy reliving the hugs and kisses he got from Helen before he jumped in the saddle. He simply rode at a comfortable trot, a huge smile splashed across his face. They were in Eureka the next day, and the first thing Amos did was write Helen a long letter, promising to turn in his badge just as soon as he found his replacement.

There was a welcoming back of sorts. More along the lines of, glad you got that bastard, that was some kind of storm, eh? And, Mrs. Sloan's dog ate my chicken. What are you going to do about that? Corcoran and Lindstrom compared notes and the acting sheriff made his way to Ed Connor's home.

"You had to kill him, Corcoran. He didn't leave you no choice. Judge will tell you the same thing." Corcoran was sitting on a chair next to Ed Connor's bed. Maryann Soto sat on the other side of the bed holding the sheriff's hand. Corcoran nodded at seeing that, looked into her smiling face, and then to Connor, who immediately tried to frown and snarl at the same time.

"It must be something in the air," Corcoran chuckled. "First my deputy, now my boss. Was plannin' on the free lunch at the Bonanza, but better hold off on that. Might run into Cindy Payton over there. And if what you've got is catching, well ..."

He ducked the wildly swung fist thrown by Connor and laughed at the fake surprised look from Maryann. "Glad you're feeling better, Sheriff," he said, laughing and walking out of the bedroom. He could hear laughter from the two before he reached the front door. *Good for them. They'll be good for each other and Connor will be one of those sheriffs who delegates most of the difficult jobs to his chief deputy, better known around these parts as, Corcoran, Terrence Corcoran.*

He was still laughing when he ran into Toby Smith, the resident deputy from Palisade. "Got bad news, Corcoran. Silas Arnold escaped, killed deputy Jenkins, stole his horse."

"You ain't gonna tell me he's riding back this way.

Can't be that dumb."

"Well, dumb he is, and riding this way he is. People keep trying to say that he has something hidden somewhere near here. There's more to it than that. He's spent his time telling everybody that he's gonna kill you and Amos White as soon as he's free. He's free, Corcoran.

"You've been chasing that gang of rustlers all over the county. I don't believe that he's looking for something besides you. Right now, I believe he's holed up in the Diamond Mountains, planning your execution."

"So Hank Whipple was right worrying about whether the Palisade jail could hold someone like Silas Arnold. How was it Jenkins got killed. He's been a deputy a long time, Toby. I can't believe he'd get careless with a known killer."

"No, the jailer got careless and Jenkins walked in as Arnold was busting out. Already had a weapon in hand and simply shot him dead. Carried old man Nelson to the edge of town and just dropped him in the mud. He got his head bashed in hard but will live."

Corcoran remembered how he always wondered whether or not the Dupree gang and the rustlers were connected, and all those thoughts came back. *Owens was talking about Dupree being in prison with a rustler. Wouldn't that be something if it was Silas Arnold. How does*

Colonel Cornell fit into all this?

"Those mountains are summer range for the valley ranchers, and that means a lot of line camps and shacks where outlaws can hide. About sixty miles or so along that range." Corcoran led Smith to the office and called out to Ed Lindstrom. "Dupree and his gang were holed up in a line shack and surely Arnold would know where many of them would be." He was muttering when Lindstrom came out from the cell area. "The Diamond Range is pure wilderness, excellent summer range, and has millions of possible hidey holes." He was talking to himself more than to Toby smith when Lindstrom came in.

"Do you have that Johnny Lewis behind bars back there?" He got a yes back and motioned for Toby Smith to have some coffee.

"You bring people with you?" Smith shook his head, and Corcoran shook his head, too. "Well, I have an idea, so just sit tight for a few minutes. Got a seriously stupid kid in jail back there who just might have some answers for us. Wish you'd brought a posse."

"Didn't have time. Wanted to be on Arnold's trail. You got far more people here to draw from than I have in Palisade."

"Guess you're right. Be back in a minute." He started into the back where the cells were to talk with

Johnny Lewis and turned to Smith. "Did Arnold ever mention anyone named Dupree or Owens? Can't get it out of my mind that this is all connected."

"The gang that blew up the train? Don't think he mentioned any names. One thing I learned by accident, though. Jonas Holiday was the man Arnold used to get rustled cattle out of the valley. Might want to pass that along to Amos. Shooting him stopped that activity."

"Speaking of that, I'm losing Amos. Pass the word up and down the valley that I'm looking for deputies."

CHAPTER NINETEEN

The line shack sat toward the back of a small stream fed glade, surrounded by tall pine, cedar, and spruce trees. Fir trees, Douglas and White, were mixed in with the others. Smoke curled from the slightly askew chimney, and three horses were standing quietly in a brush corral. The three men inside were drinking coffee laced with whiskey, and playing cards.

"There's gonna be a hell of a posse searchin' for you, Silas. You shoulda run north when you had the chance." The big man had his arm in a sling, and his anger could almost be felt. "I'll ride with you, though, just so I can shoot Amos White fifteen times. My arm will never be the same because of him," Jonas Holiday said.

"You have your priorities," the third man said, "and I have mine. I'll work hand in glove with you two killing Amos White and Terrence Corcoran, and you work with me taking out Peter Bridges and that vault of his filled with money." He sat back in his chair looking at kings over aces and slipped another hundred dollars onto the table. "I call."

Silas Arnold and Jonas Holiday flipped their cards and Colonel Buford S. Cornell enjoyed lighting his cigar. "Read 'em, gentlemen," he said showing his hand. He raked in the table and smiled. "Young Johnny Lewis thought he was working for that fool Dupree, who left him out in the cold. He gave me his set of keys before he was arrested and I made duplicates. We can waltz into that bank anytime we want."

Cornell's frustration level was showing. He was sure that Dupree and Owens would be the ones to crack that bank open. He had always had a plan, the perfect plan he said, often, but never had the men to pull it off. Dupree let him down and now, he had Silas Arnold and Jonas Holiday. "I'm offering you the gift of a lifetime, gentlemen."

"You might have something, Cornell. Make our attempt on the bank a little sloppy and Corcoran and White will be running hard to catch us up." Silas Arnold never noticed that when all the hands were showing, there were five aces. Cornell covered that little problem with all the money he raked in. "Really want to shoot that big bastard," Arnold said.

"Yeah," Jonas Holiday snickered. "We'll be catching them up. I like that idea. Let's fill this plan out and work on it. Open the bank's vault and kill us a sheriff and his deputy. Best idea I've heard in a long time. Might have to give up sellin' other people's cattle." Only he and Arnold chuckled. "You sure those keys you made will work?"

Colonel Cornell scowled. He didn't like being questioned by someone not smart enough to pull the colonel's boots on. He pulled a ring of keys from his coat pocket and rattled them about. "Sure as the day is long, Mr. Holiday. These are Johnny Lewis's keys. I gave him the ones I made just in case I wasn't my normal perfect. Let's have a drink."

The plan was developed over the next few hours, two bottles of good bourbon were consumed, and the men called it a night. Cornell spread his bedroll in the three-sided barn, next to a blazing fire, and the other two had cots inside the shack. Cornell made the five mile ride to town at sunrise. He saw Corcoran, Lindstrom, White, and Toby Smith ride out as he stepped off his horse in front of the Bonanza Club.

"You boys lookin' for Silas Arnold aren't gonna find him," he snickered. "But we are sure as hell gonna find you." He had a pocket full of money taken from

Arnold and Holiday, visions of even more to be taken from Peter Bridges' bank, and ambled into the Bonanza Club. "Cards were with me last night, let's see how warm they are this morning."

He saw the enchanting Betty Cord at the bar talking with Jack Munson. "Good morning, Colonel," she said with a smile. "I've been looking for a chance to have a conversation with you. My father served, was a major, I believe. Illinois regulars."

"Most of my work was undercover, I'm afraid. Didn't have much contact with regulars. Would you join me for breakfast. I understand you're quite a seamstress." Betty joined the colonel just as Terrence Corcoran had asked.

"What were you doing at the bank last night, Corcoran? I thought with Oscar Owens dead, all that would have been cleared up." Ed Lindstrom didn't miss much when he made his rounds of Eureka.

"The idea of Dupree's gang robbing the bank is cleared up, but not the idea of the bank being robbed. I don't think we're gonna have to do much riding to find Silas Arnold. He's gonna come looking for us. That idiot Johnny Lewis told me about another plan, this one home-grown."

They rode down to the valley floor and the Eureka

and Palisade Railroad station to put Toby Smith on the train back to Palisade. "You see to it that Jenkins' family gets that letter from Ed Connor and the money that's inside. He was a good deputy, Smith. Take care of his family."

"I will Sheriff, and thank you. Good luck catching Arnold. This isn't his first escape."

"It's sure as hell is his last," Corcoran growled. "Have a good trip and keep Palisade safe," Corcoran shook young Smith's hand. "We'll keep you advised after whatever happens takes place. Just don't trust those telegraph wires and their so-called secrecy."

"What's the plan, Sheriff?" Lindstrom asked as they rode off from the depot. "What did that kid Lewis tell you?"

"Let's ride north along the main road and see if we find any fairly recent tracks leading off into the Diamond Mountains. It seems that our own Colonel Buford Cornell is planning to rob the bank, and I'll betcha aces over kings that he's going to be working with Silas Arnold and Jonas Holiday."

"How the hell did you learn all that? My God, Corcoran, Arnold's only been broke out for a few days, and I shot Holiday," Amos White said.

"Yup, you did indeed shoot Holiday, but while we were fighting our way out of the mountains, Holiday came to Eureka and fell in with Cornell. Seems Holiday was the man who helped Arnold rustle the cattle in the valley. He was the man who helped set up the sales for the gang and knew Arnold would try to escape."

"Yeah, but he wanted to hang him."

"He did," Corcoran said. "So he wouldn't tell about Holiday's part in all of it."

"Good partner, eh?" Amos White chuckled. "Why come to Eureka?" White was confused. "Hank Whipple fired him, why not ride to another valley and look for work?"

"Came here to wait for you to come back so he could kill you is what I heard." He checked to make sure Amos White understood what he said. "Our Colonel Cornell was trying to help Dupree, had his own plans for the bank job, but Dupree wouldn't let him in. He's a sweet talking liar, and Jonas Holiday isn't the smartest man you've ever met, and now the killer Silas Arnold is in the party. We got us a real mess."

"How do you know all this, Corcoran?" Lindstrom was as confused as Amos White.

"I have inside information from a source who will remain unknown for the time being. But as for the bank robbery? Johnny Lewis gave me details. Seems Cornell wanted to be in with Dupree and talked Lewis into letting him reproduce the bank's keys. We got those keys when we arrested the kid. I went to the bank to make sure Peter Bridges hadn't changed the locks. Lewis's keys wouldn't work.

"Cornell did a bum job reproducing them and kept the real ones and gave the bad ones back to Lewis. Nobody found about that because that dumb kid was arrested." All three men had to laugh at that. "There's going to be an attempted bank robbery in the next few days, gentlemen, and we're gonna be there to stop it."

They rode about eight or ten miles north and found that many riders had ridden off into the Diamond Mountains since that last big storm. There fresh and old prints on half a dozen trails they passed. "Didn't learn much on that ride, boys. Let's head back to town. Not a word now, to anyone, about what we know. Mr. White, I want you to concentrate on your own personal safety. There are men looking for you. Oh, and, find your replacement."

"I will, Sheriff," he said. *You bet I'm gonna keep myself safe with that pretty girl waiting for me.*

They took care of their horses and left them in the small corral behind the jail. "A long cold glass of beer awaits," Corcoran said. "Why don't you two join me?"

Colonel Buford S. Cornell walked into the Carter Dry Goods late in the afternoon. "Ah, Miss Cord, it's so nice that you're helping to take care of the Carter family while Henry is in jail. Will you join me for a glass of wine when you close up shop?" He now was playing the part of a southern gentleman and Betty Cord had a hard time holding in the giggles.

"I would be delighted, Colonel. Absolutely delighted. It's so nice to have such a distinguished and intelligent man to converse with." She had to turn her head, pretend to do anything so she wouldn't be looking at the man. "There are far too many rowdy men in this mining camp." Betty Cord had her red hair swept up in a bun. "I'll be closing shortly, sir. At the Bonanza Club?" She let the bun loose and the hair cascaded about her shoulders. She could hear Colonel Cornell draw in his breath and almost chuckled.

"I swear what I'm looking at is a princess from a Virginia plantation before the war. Oh, that war devastated the south. You were too young to know what it was."

Betty grew up on a Minnesota farm, had never been further south than St. Louis, and just smiled back at the preening gentleman. "Yes, I was," she said, casting her eyes toward the floor. "It must have been awful." Her father was dirt-farmer, not a major in the union army, but the good colonel would never know that.

"I wonder if I might ask your indulgence, dear lady?

I will soon be rather wealthy, as you know," and he gave her a quick wink and smile. "Your help getting me those arrival schedules have been most helpful. I'm meeting with my partners late tonight and we will establish the exact date and time for our little adventure."

"Oh, that's wonderful, Colonel. I'm excited," she said. She reached out and touched his sleeve, smiling into his face. She held in the revulsion of the move and was amazed to see the old reprobate almost weaken from her touch.

"We'll make a fine couple in the hotels of Europe, my dear." Cornell tipped his hat by way of the crown of his cane, the one with the carved ivory eagle, and shiny brass fittings, and smiled at what he hoped would soon be his wife. He all but marched down the street to the saloon and found a table near the piano where he and Betty Cord would be able to talk. He had much to tell the lady, and if things went the way he wanted them to, he would offer himself to her on a permanent basis.

Betty watched him walk down the street and knew she had to get the new information to Corcoran. "Damn it, he wants supper with me and I want, need, to be with Terrence. I'll drink his wine and then call off supper," she fumed. It took just minutes to close up the shop.

Cornell was sitting at his table, cigar lit, and reached

in his frock coat inside pocket, made sure the ring in its velvet lined box was still there. He signaled for a bottle of wine and two glasses, and watched the evening crowd come to life. "Ah, yes, our fine acting sheriff and his disreputable deputies are making themselves known to the citizenry," he murmured. "At least two of you will be dead this time next week and I'll be sailing from San Francisco for the east, and then, Europe."

Corcoran, White, and Lindstrom were at the bar with cold beer and Corcoran whispered, "Check the mirror and see who's watching us. Don't make it obvious, but the good colonel can't take his eyes off our backs."

"He's expecting a guest. There are two glasses on the table. I didn't know he drank wine," Lindstrom said.

"He doesn't. Betty Cord does," Corcoran chuckled.

"Your unnamed source," Amos White said. "How long has she been working for you, Corcoran?" The big Irisher just chuckled and called for three more beers. "You have your ways, Mr. White, and I have mine."

Colonel Cornell jumped to his feet when Betty came in and walked up to their table. "Miss Cord," he said, pulled a chair back for her, and got her seated properly. "It's a lovely evening, isn't it?"

"Clear and cold tonight, I'm afraid I'm going to

have to pass on your suggestion of a buggy ride. Too cold for me. I'll sit by the fire and read to the Carter children, I think."

He wouldn't allow her to see his disappointment, and instead suggested that maybe they could enjoy supper together. The ring burned in its little box, the colonel burned with frustration. She turned down supper, too, but they talked for several minutes. It was animated at times, Betty laughing softly from time to time, and Cornell seeming to be very business like.

Corcoran walked up to the table. "Good evening, Miss Cord. Colonel. It's going to be cold tonight."

"It is cold, now," Cornell said. He didn't stand and offer his hand, but Corcoran was ignoring him anyway, and took Betty's in his hand. He kissed it gently.

"How is Carter's mother and children?"

"They're doing well, Sheriff. I understand you caught that train robber. Congratulations. And some cattle rustlers, too?"

"Indeed," Cornell snuffed.

"Yes, but it seems one of the rustlers has escaped, killed one of my deputies in Palisade. Don't know where he might run to. Every sheriff in Nevada has been notified. He'll be caught and hung for the murder." He was looking straight into Cornell's eyes when he said that.

Cornell gave another humph, drank his wine in one swallow and stood. "I believe I'll have supper. Good night, Miss Cord. Acting Sheriff." He tried to swagger as he walked toward the restaurant in the back of the Bonanza Club, and Corcoran noticed White and Lindstrom followed him with their eyes in the mirror.

"We need to talk, Corcoran. I found out a lot of what he's planning."

"Sure can't do it here, and can't be seen either. Come by the office in half an hour or so. Make sure someone knows your coming to give Carter a report on his children." He bowed, nodded, and walked back to the bar.

"I think we're safe for tonight, gentlemen. Make your rounds and be in the office early. The hit might just be coming our way very soon."

Betty and Corcoran were alone in the office and she told him what Cornell had told her. "He's so sure of himself, Terrence. He frightens me. Those men he's working with are killers."

"Yes they are, and you're right to be frightened. Cornell is a stupid pig and those men will kill him as soon as they are clear of town. They might even kill him before the job. From what you've told me, they are more interested in killing young White and me than robbing the bank.

"If he asks you to participate in any way, don't. Men like Silas Arnold and Jonas Holiday wouldn't hesitate to use you as a hostage for a safe get away."

"He did suggest that it might help if I were at the bank as kind of a diversion. Oh, my," she whispered.

Corcoran gathered her up in his arms and could feel her shaking from fright. "Stay as far away from that bank as you can," he said. He gently brushed her hair from her eyes, and they kissed and kissed, and kissed some more. "Go home before I forget I'm a gentleman, Betty. We'll work toward being alone more often, eh?"

"I don't want to go home, Corcoran. I don't, but I know I have to," she kissed him long and slow one more time, let him help her into a winter's coat, and slipped out the door. *I could stay in his arms forever if he'd let me. Damn you, Corcoran.*

Terrence Corcoran paced around the little office trying to piece together everything Betty Cord had told him, and let her lingering aroma and the taste of those delightful lips mingle with his thoughts. "Damn fine lady," he murmured. "I wonder how long Colonel Cornell has been thinking about robbing old man Bridges' bank? How did he know about Dupree and company and I didn't? How is it he is tangled up with Arnold? At least I know there was a connection between Dupree and Arnold."

Colonel Buford S. Cornell went out of his way to meet and get as close as possible to every newcomer to Eureka, Corcoran remembered. "That must be how he does it. He inserts himself in their lives, gets too close, wants to know everything and goes out of his way to insinuate that he is an expert on whatever the newcomer is interested in." He had a complete conversation going with the exception of not getting answers back.

His pacing and lively commentary continued for some time with no benefit of answers to the questions. "Silas Arnold, known rustler from many years ago gets out of jail and resumes his trade. Dupree and his cohorts arrive to rob the bank. Cornell seems to know all of them. It doesn't make sense."

He paced around room for some time and then it hit him. "Arnold was rustling in this valley, and he must have run into Cornell many times, heard many times how he would be able to rob the bank, and passed that on to Dupree. Dupree then knew who to contact when he and the gang got here."

He sat down at the desk, filled his coffee cup with brandy, and spent the next half hour putting it all down on paper. He signed the document, slipped it into an envelope, and addressed it to Ed Connor. He smiled, sadly, wrote on the envelope, "To be delivered in the event of my death."

CHAPTER TWENTY

Lindstrom was walking up and down the main street in Eureka late, shaking the doors to make sure shop owners locked up or that others had got in, and saw Colonel Cornell ride slowly out of town. He dashed to the corral behind the jail, saddled up, and followed. Where the hell would he be going this time of night? Even blow-hard colonels don't go pleasure riding after midnight.

Cornell led Lindstrom down the canyon out of town and onto the road north through Diamond Valley. It was a cold night, no wind and no moon, and they rode for almost five miles before turning east into the foothills of the Diamond Range. "He's taking me right to the outlaw camp," Lindstrom murmured. He was back many hundreds of yards, staying as much in deep shadow as possible. Never once did he see Cornell check his back trail.

Most of the snow from the last big storm was melted and they were riding across the top of frozen mud and it was noisy. "Not often I wish for wind but it would help tonight," he whispered. They rode into a wide canyon, crossing a small creek several times. Lindstrom pulled up suddenly when Cornell called out. He couldn't see whoever or whatever he was calling to.

"Jonas, don't shoot, it's me, Cornell," the colonel hollered.

"Ride in slow and alone, Colonel. You shouldn't be here."

Lindstrom got off his horse and tied it off to some willows along the creek, and slowly walked toward the voices. The cabin was hidden in an all but closed off copse of pine trees. There was no light coming from the windows or doors, but he could see smoke from the chimney. He was much closer than he wanted to be and knelt down in the frozen mud to listen.

"We said we weren't going to be meeting, Colonel. You better not have brought the law. Get in the cabin and hurry." Jonas Holiday held a shotgun and used it to motion Cornell in. "Silas, take a walk around out there, will you? This fool might have been followed. Damn, that's why we told you not to come out here."

Silas Arnold grumbled but did as he was told,

grabbed his rifle and slipped outside. Holiday closed the shutters and lit a lamp.

"We said not to meet until we had all the information," Cornell said. He was angry at the way Holiday was talking to him and wasn't going to let him get away with it. This was his job and his way to the splendors of Europe. "Well, that"s why I'm here. I have all the information we need, dates, times, and amounts. Don't let that temper of yours foul up what is going to make us rich. There are four big mines in this county and all of them pay on the same day. Bridges' bank has that payroll in the vault right now."

He had been working with Holiday for three years, relaying information on herd movements and gold shipments. When Dupree showed up with information that Silas Arnold was about to be released from prison, the idea of using rustling to draw off attention on the bank became the hot topic. Holiday was making good money working with the rustlers, but not anywhere near what would be available in that bank vault.

Cornell was a blowhard, believed most of the lies and cockeyed stories he told, had great confidence in himself despite never having accomplished anything he took credit for. All of these people came together simply because he just happened to be at the bar in Eureka. All of them, to some degree, believed that he did know everything there was to know about that bank.

Lindstrom saw enough and slipped back to his horse, mounted, and let the horse pick its way out of the canyon. He had gone about fifty yards when Silas Arnold saw him and yelled out.

"Hold it up right there, stranger." He brought the rifle up and fired one shot. The bullet tore through Lindstrom's heavy wool coat, ripped out a piece of good shoulder meat, but didn't knock the deputy from the saddle.

"Hiyah!" Lindstrom sunk the spurs deep and the horse was at full speed, racing out of the canyon, across the creek several times and onto the main road in minutes. Arnold fired that big lever-action rifle three more times, missing with every shot. Lindstrom never let up. He was laid out across the horse's neck and raced the five miles back at a full gallop, sliding the horse to a stop in front of the sheriff's office. He was out of the saddle and in the door in a flash, scaring Corcoran into dropping a full cup of hot coffee.

"What the hell got you all fired up, Lindstrom? Damn, good brandy in that spilled coffee, boy."

"I found the gang's hideout," Lindstrom blurted out. "Coffee, brandy, I'll tell you all about it. Look, that's a bullet hole in my coat. look." He was yelling as fast as he could get the words out. He tried to get out of his coat and couldn't. That arm was hurt more than he knew.

"All right, calm down," Corcoran almost chuckled. He poured them both some coffee, laced both with brandy, and told Lindstrom to sit down. "Got shot at, eh? Let's get you out of that coat and see how bad. Tell me all about it while I patch you up. I love a good story."

He listened and worked on the wound. The bullet clipped the edge of his collar bone and ripped through some meat. "Gonna hurt for some time, Lindstrom. I'm glad you followed that old fool but I sure wish there had been time to grab one of us to go with you." With Lindstrom's description, Corcoran knew exactly where Cornell had gone, knew the cabin, in fact.

"Any way they might have recognized you?"

"No. There ain't no moon, I was thirty yards or so away and riding out when whoever it was shot me. I'm sure no one could identify me or my horse. This wound might give it away, though come sunrise."

"Let's plan on taking a ride after the sun comes up," Corcoran said. "You, me, and Amos White. Sure wish Sandy McAuliff was well. According to Betty, they're planning on hitting that bank in the next couple of days. Cornell was probably at the cabin to wrap up their plans.

"Get a couple hours of sleep, meet me at the Bonanza for breakfast, and we'll ride out. I want to talk with Jack Munson in the morning, too."

"What the hell." Jonas Holiday jumped up from the table and ran to the cabin door at the sound of a rifle. "What're you shooting at?" He yelled at Silas Arnold. "You okay?"

"I'm fine, damn it. Somebody lurking out there. Caught him riding off and took some shots, but I guess I missed in the dark." He looked around for Cornell. "Where's that colonel? He brought somebody with him. He needs killin', Holiday."

Colonel Cornell followed Holiday out of the cabin. "I didn't bring nobody and nobody followed me," Cornell growled. "And you ain't gonna be killin' nobody, Arnold. Your shootin' at somebody is sure to bring the law."

"You're sure he was alone? Don't need any more surprises around here." Jonas Holiday rubbed his sore shoulder, kicked some mud, and cussed.

"Only tracks I could see were his and the colonel's. I swear those tracks sure do look like you two rode in together. That man brings the law back, you die before they do. You're too slick with your words, want people to think you know everything. Well, you don't know dung, Colonel."

This had grown meaner than Cornell anticipated, both Arnold and Holiday were known killers, and he never did really see any action in the war. "I'm calling you out, Cornell. You brought someone up here." Silas Arnold held that rifle at the ready, Cornell could see the hammer was back on the powerful Winchester, knew his heavy coat was fastened and he could no more go for his weapon than fly.

"You ain't gonna shoot a man that can't get at his gun to protect himself," Cornell almost whimpered.

"Maybe I am," Arnold Snickered. "Well, then, Colonel, open up that coat and let's just see what kind man you think you are. Here, Holiday, take the rifle and we'll settle this with handguns. I like watching the bullet tear into a man's heart, rip through a man's head. Before you die, Colonel, who did you bring to see our little party?"

"Didn't bring nobody," Cornell said, slowly getting out of his coat. He let it drop to the frozen mud and immediately went for his Colt. He had his fingers closed on the handle, had the hammer halfway back and the gun part of the way out of the holster when two heavy slugs tore through his chest, one from each man standing in front of him. A Colt smoked in one hand, a Winchester in another.

"That was good, Holiday. I thought you said White ruined your shoulder." Silas Arnold was laughing and Holiday seemed surprised that he was able to level that rifle and fire as quick as Arnold.

"By golly, it was," Holiday grinned. "Let's get that fool out of sight and figure out what to do. I hate it when good plans get screwed up. I want White dead. That bank was just something else."

"Yeah, it was. I want Corcoran dead. There is a lot of money in that bank and we do know how to get it, thanks to our dead partner," Arnold laughed. "Can't pass up a gift like that."

They dragged Cornell's body into the lean-to near the brush corral, got his horse undressed and in the corral and slipped back into the shack. They went through his pockets and got that ring of keys, smiling at each other. "If that was the law that followed the colonel, we gotta get out of here, and I mean right now," Holiday said. "Move into the hills south of town and plan on taking out that bank. We can be at a line shack I know before dawn if we leave out now."

All they took with them were bedrolls, coffee, and some smoked meat. "After we hit the bank, which way is best to get away?" Silas Arnold knew the country north and west of Eureka like the back of his hand but had been in prison for several years, wasn't sure of how things might be today.

"I'm riding for Ward and south to Mexico," Jonas Holiday said. "Just as soon ride alone, though."

"Yup, be best if we split up. I'm heading for San Francisco," Silas Arnold said. "Women and whiskey on the menu," he laughed. "You ever been there, Holiday?"

"Nope. Too many people. Give me open range, high mountains, and wide sky. Don't much care for people. Find me a wide valley in Mexico, a pretty señorita, and barrels of tequila, and I'll be one happy gringo. But I want my share of Amos White before I go. Shot me down in cold blood he did. Gonna kill him and laugh in his face as I do."

"Corcoran's mine," Arnold snapped. "Nice and slow for him. Gunnin' him down is too good. I'm using my knife and I'm gonna give a lesson in carving when I do." Both men were laughing as they rode through the late night.

Cindy Payton was still working on getting the stoves fired up when Corcoran slipped into her kitchen. "Mornin', beautiful. Gonna be three of us at table number one, sweetheart."

She wrapped her arms around his neck and hugged him tight. "Did you hear about Maryann Soto? Did you?"

"I guess not, Cindy. What about Maryann Soto." He smiled, patted her little bottom and reached for the coffee pot. "Last I heard she was nursing the sheriff."

"Well, she's doing more than that," she snickered, then blushed. "I mean, I didn't mean, oh, hell, Corcoran. You got me all riled. She's gonna marry Ed Connor. Marry him!"

"I think that's wonderful for Ed. He needs a good woman," Corcoran said. "Maryann will take good care of our sheriff."

"Humph," Cindy said. "You need a good woman, Corcoran. Somebody to take good care of you."

"I suppose you have someone in mind?"

"Of course I do. You need a good woman like me to take care of you," and she wrapped her arms around him again. He patted her bottom again and walked out to the table to meet Lindstrom and White.

"I'll give that some thought," he laughed. He detoured to the bar when he saw barman Jack Munson wiping it down, trying not to pay any attention to the storm of words coming from the kitchen.

"Mornin' Jack. Got a couple of quick questions for you. Can you remember seeing that outlaw Dupree or his partner Oscar Owens around town sometime before they showed up for good?"

"I've been wonderin' the same thing, Terence, lad.

That bad one, Owens, he and Colonel Cornell were plenty close and I'm sure that this was Owens' first visit. But Dupree, I'm thinkin' he's been in town before. Maybe I've got it turned around and it was Owens here before." He reached back to the shelf behind and pulled out one of the posters Corcoran passed out.

"This is what caught my attention, Terrence. Dupree and Silas Arnold were in prison at the same time in Denver and got out about the same time. It was Owens who was here and met with Cornell a couple of months ago."

"You're a gem, Mr. Munson. A gem." Corcoran walked over to the table where Amos White and Ed Lindstrom were waiting. "Gentlemen," he said. "Up for a good hard ride this morning? How's that arm?"

"Sore as hell, but ready to ride. It's only about five miles." Lindstrom moved his shoulder around in a circle, tried not to groan, but did try to smile.

CHAPTER TWENTY-ONE

"The cabin's about a mile in, Corcoran. Looks to me, though, that at least three horses rode out of this canyon in the last few hours. One of them would have been mine."

With all the mud and having to cross the creek, fresh prints stood out in the early morning light. Frost glittered in the bright sun and shadows were deep and dark. "I think they've fled the nest." Amos White was scowling, riding point for the group. "But if we see your prints, Mr. Lindstrom, and two others, that means somebody is still at that cabin."

"No question, Amos," Corcoran said. "Let's see what they left us." Even though the signs said the cabin would be empty, they rode in with caution and tied off near the brush corral. Corcoran and Lindstrom walked toward the cabin and White moved toward the lean-to. "That arm hurtin'? You got a pained look, Ed."

"Yeah. I just gave it a bump. I'll be fine." The men were off their horses, giving the grounds around the cabin and corral a going over. There were rolling hills spread out in a wide spectrum, plenty of water, and good grass. A buckaroo watching a summer's herd would have an easy time.

"Something was dragged in here recently," Ed Lindstrom said. "Something with boots and spurs." He moved into the shaded, three-sided shack and almost stumbled over the colonel's frozen corpse. "Looks like Cornell played his last con game, Sheriff."

They finished their search of the area, found a few items that were left but nothing of any consequence. It was difficult getting Cornell's frozen body tied to his horse for the ride back to Eureka, but they were on the trail within half an hour.

"Did they high-tail it, Corcoran? Or is that bank job still in the works?" Amos White asked.

"Arnold and Holiday came to kill us, not rob a bank. It was Cornell got them all twisted up about the bank. Neither one is smart enough to tie a knot, so I would guess they'll try for the bank." All three were laughing as they reined up in front of the sheriff's office. It was a cold day in the high mountain desert, but there wasn't any wind and no clouds ushering in another brutal storm system.

"I thought maybe you boys had left the county," Sandy McAuliff said, stepping out of the office. "Come on in. I got it nice and warm for you."

"Glad you're feeling better," Corcoran said. "That's Cornell draped over the horse. Amos, will you walk that horse over to the funeral house? Then come back here. We all got some serious talking to do. A bunch of what-ifs in my head right now." Corcoran's anger hadn't eased since Toby Smith told him about Jenkins' death in Paradise. To know his killer was somewhere close brought his blood to the boiling point. *Silas Arnold killed a lawman working for me and I'm gonna see him dead or swimming in irons.*

"I tell you, Arnold, the only reason a lawman would have been following Cornell is if they already knew something. He's just an old guy likes to hear himself talk. Why would they follow him unless they knew something." Holiday had a fire lit in the line shack on the side of a hill two miles south of Eureka.

"He gave us the keys to get in," Holiday chuckled. "Gave us information about the locks, the vault, and the schedules. Did that loud mouth of his also tell somebody else? Can't just ride in and do the job, either. Everybody in town knows what I look like, probably remember you."

Of the two men, Holiday had the quicker mind and Arnold just nodded at what he was saying. "We'll do it the way Cornell outlined it. Get in the bank before sunrise, and when old man Bridges shows up, force him to unlock the vault, kill him, and ride off. It would be nice, though, to draw that damn deputy in and kill the bastard." Holiday was pacing around the small shack, poured some coffee.

"Having a poke full will be nice, too."

"Yeah, it would," Arnold said. "Let's just follow the original plan and hope the law shows up so we can kill 'em. Let's be in the bank at four tomorrow morning. Cornell said Bridges gets there at six sharp every morning, and we'll be waiting. Ain't gonna be nobody wandering around at that time of the morning to see us. When we're runnin' out, who cares if they see us."

Corcoran found Betty Ford alone in Henry Carter's store and wanted to make sure she had told him everything that Cornell had told her. "They gunned him down in cold blood, sweetheart, and rode off. I don't believe they're gonna give up all that bank money. I'm sure they'll break in soon, probably tomorrow. Go over everything Cornell told you one more time, just in case something slipped by."

"He was a slimy old man, but even so, I'm sorry he's dead," she said. She went over the plan one more time, detailing everything. "He was going to go to the bank an hour or so before Bridges shows up, bundle up what was normally left out in the cashier's drawers, and wait for Bridges so he could open the vault. It just always sounded too pat for me."

"Nothing else you can think of?" She shook her head and shrugged her shoulders. "Well, with Cornell dead and Arnold and Holiday loose somewhere, I'd guess they'll hit the bank in the morning. Not a word of this to anyone, Betty. You know that," he said. He gathered her up and gave her a long kiss.

"You going to have all your deputies with you?"

"Only me and Amos White. Ed Lindstrom's shoulder hurts like hell, so I'm gonna have him outside with a rifle in case they break free. All our horses will be saddled and ready, too. Just in case we have to chase 'em."

They kissed a few more times and Corcoran headed back to the office. "I wonder just how many of the strangers that ride through our little town have run into Colonel Cornell and been intrigued with his ideas of robbing the bank? Just what did Dupree and Arnold talk about in jail and how did Oscar Owens get connected? Owens and Dupree rode together, right," he murmured, sorting it all out.

"This damn thing is funny, Mr. Lindstrom," Corcoran said after pouring some coffee and settling in at his desk. "The entire Dupree gang is dead. The man behind the Dupree gang robbing the Eureka Bank is dead. And we have two people who only got involved after the fact, planning to rob the bank. What a mess."

"Me and Sandy McAuliff have a plan, Corcoran. I'll be across from the bank near the drug store, to the west and Sandy will be across the street near the cobbler shop to the east. They can't get out of town without passing by one of us, and we're both crack shots."

"And you're both busted up. It's a good idea but don't go getting yourself killed doin' it," Corcoran chuckled. "That's an order from your acting Sheriff."

"I'm more worried about Amos than myself. He's got Helen Whipple on his mind, Corcoran."

"I know. I'll take him for a cold beer and have a chat. I need someone in the bank with me, and neither you nor Sandy are able. Got somebody in mind, spill it out." *Don't want Amos to have to be with me but I don't have anyone else. Wish Sonny Rafferty were here. I'll talk to the boy and make sure his head is screwed on tight.*

Corcoran found Amos at the bar having a beer and talking with Jack Munson, the barman. "Let's have a chat, Amos." They walked over to a table by the window, away from the crowd at the bar. "We'll be in the bank tonight, waiting for Arnold and Holiday and it could get mighty dangerous mighty quick. You cannot be one hundred percent if you're thinking about something other than stopping the two outlaws."

"You mean if I'm thinking about Helen Whipple? I know, and it's been bothering me. What we're about to do is why she doesn't want me to be a lawman, and what I'm thinking about is why you don't think I'd be a good lawman. Sittin' in that dark bank waiting for them yahoos to show up and not thinking about Helen is gonna be more than hard, Corcoran.

"I want to do the right thing, and that would be to sit in the dark and wait for those outlaws, nab them, and call it a day. I won't let you down, Sheriff. Don't you be worrying about me and take your mind off what we're there for."

Corcoran had to laugh right out at what Amos said, whacked him across the shoulders and motioned for Munson to bring a couple more beers. "You are one fine sumbitch, Mr. White. I wish you'd never met the girl, but since you have, I want to wish you all the best. After we both keep our minds on the job," he laughed.

It was three in the morning when Corcoran led his men out of the office and down the main street of Eureka. The only lights came from the Bonanza Club and they didn't run into anyone out walking. He dropped Lindstrom off at the apothecary and left Sandy Mc-Cauliff off at the boot shop. "We'll go in the back door, Amos. That's where Arnold and Holiday will come. Bridges always leaves one lamp burning low in the vestibule, so we will be able to see our way around."

They had planted their saddled horses off the main street but close enough that they could run to them quickly. "Never been in a closed bank," Amos said. "Almost spooky." Even at a whisper, his voice seemed loud. The hardwood floor along with oak and marble walls echoed with each step they took or word they said.

"You hide behind the big desk over there," Corcoran said. "I'll slip behind the cashier's cage. "No quarter. I'll call out to stop. Shoot at the slightest move, Amos. Don't give either man a half-second or he'll shoot you for sure."

They only had about twenty minutes to wait, but to Amos White, it was five hours. He couldn't stop thinking about Helen Whipple, the Rocking W, maybe even children. It was the slightest scratching at the back door that brought him back to reality instantly. The Colt, fully cocked, was in his hand, his eyes were glued to the back door, and he watched it slowly swing open.

CHAPTER TWENTY-TWO

"Ready?" Jonas Holiday whispered, slowly turning the key they took from Colonel Cornell. In the early morning quiet, he could hear the scraping as the bolt withdrew. He turned the knob and let the door gently swing open. The two outlaws looked at each other, their guns drawn, and Holiday motioned Arnold to go in first.

Arnold wanted to shake it off but stepped into the open vestibule of the Eureka Bank. Their horses were loosely tied off just around the corner, ready for their run out of town. Bridges wouldn't see the horses, coming from the other direction.

Arnold stepped inside and motioned for Holiday to come on, which he did. Corcoran watched Holiday take one step in and turn to close the door. When he heard it click, he hollered out, "Stop right there. Freeze."

Arnold whirled to face the voice and brought his weapon up. It sounded like one massive explosion as three heavy handguns went off all but simultaneously. Holiday turned and ran to the door, yanked it open and raced for his horse. Arnold died from two wounds to the middle of his chest and Amos White moved quickly to make sure he was out of the fight.

"Corcoran. You okay?"

"Go after Holiday, hurry. I'll be right behind you." Corcoran knew he wouldn't be running for a long time. Arnold's shot went through his boot and through his foot. He fought to get the boot off to stem the flow of blood. *Busted half a dozen bones and ruined a fine boot, too.* He had to chuckle through the pain, got the boot off, and his foot wrapped tight.

Amos was out the door and onto the back street when he heard two shots, one from a rifle, one from a handgun, and ran around the building to the main street. Sandy McAuliff yelled at him that Holiday was riding north and Lindstrom was on his tail. "Good," Amos White murmured. Their horses were that way, too, and he sprinted up the street.

He turned to where their horses were tied and heard two more shots less than a hundred yards off. He was mounted and found Lindstrom on his knees in the mud. "You hurt?"

"Yeah," Ed Lindstrom shouted. "My leg's a mess. Go, he's right in front of you. Go."

White put the spurs to his big horse and raced down the street, around two buildings and out onto the rolling hills that led down to the valley floor. Holiday didn't take the road, he worked through a couple of side streets and was out of town, going cross country, more north than west. It was a horrible rock and brush strewn side hill they were racing across and down.

The early morning light was just enough to make for good running, and White spotted Holiday several hundred yards in front. Both men were running their horses at breakneck speed through stands of heavy brush and timber, great outcrops of rock, racing downhill for the main road leading north. They raced through patches of deep snow, areas of frozen mud, and grass made slick by early morning frost.

"I'm on my own chasing a killer across Nevada's open country, exactly what Helen Whipple doesn't want me to do. I'm a damn fool," Amos almost shouted. "Come on, horse. We got one job to finish and then hang up this badge." He wasn't gaining on Holiday as they weaved their way down the hill but figured once they hit the road he would.

Both men were buckaroos, spent hours chasing young, quick steers through the wilds of Nevada.

Racing through open country wasn't new, wasn't un-usual. The difference, of course, steers don't shoot at you. The distance was too far for either to think about handguns and neither was willing to try and shoot a rifle effectively at breakneck speeds.

The sun finally flooded the area and brought a touch of warmth with it but only increased the danger. "Bastard can see me now," White murmured. "Gotta get close enough to pull up and take a rifle shot. Come on, horse. Give me everything you've got." Holiday leaped the drainage ditch alongside the main road and got as low in the saddle as he could, spurring his horse unmercifully.

White made the jump with ease and gave his horse full rein. "All out, now, big boy," and touched the spurs. He rode a big ranch horse and knew that Holiday did, too. Both horses were range strong, made great circles regularly working the cattle in the high country and on the plain. This would be a long and hard race between two excellent horses ridden by two fine buckaroos. "We're gonna be at this for a while, big boy." He said racing north through bitter cold air.

They were in a long sweeping turn through a jum-ble of rocks and trees, the railroad tracks to their left, high rocks and timber to their right, when Holiday fell off his horse, rolled across the road and crawled behind a stand of pine trees.

Amos White pulled his horse up quickly, jumped from the saddle, rifle in hand, and ran to the right edge of the road, getting into the rocks. "What the hell is this all about?" He had his rifle at the ready and started moving north to find Holiday. "That horse didn't shy and Holiday's a better rider than that. He sure as hell didn't jump. Man's full of tricks."

He stayed as low as he could, moving from one out-crop to the next, using trees for cover, easing around heavy brush, and figured he was about fifty or so yards from where Holiday fell. He moved behind an outcrop that allowed him to see across to where Holiday should be. "There you are, Mister Holiday. I'm not gonna be a nice guy this time." Visions of shooting the man so as not to kill him flashed through his mind. White shook his head as he brought the rifle up.

He could see Holiday scrunched up against a tree, trying to get a rag tied around his leg. "So, either Ed or Sandy put one in you, eh? Well, you're about to get another one." Holiday had been bleeding heavy for the entire ride down the hillside and was too weak to stay in the saddle. Amos White pulled his rifle to his shoulder and took a long squeeze on the trigger, driving a heavy slug deep into Holiday's back, high and slightly to the left. Holiday lurched forward, face first in the mud.

White waited some time before moving. Holiday hadn't moved since being driven into the mud and rocks. "Easy does it, Amos lad," he murmured. More than one buckaroo had walked up on a dead snake only to get bitten. He made his way to what he hoped would be a dead Mr. Holiday, but keeping rocks and trees between them as much as possible, just in case.

A slug from his Winchester, at this distance, should have torn things up good, White knew, but on the other hand, Holiday was strong and wily. Amos moved so that he came up on the man from behind, his handgun at the ready. "One little twitch, Holiday, that's all I'm asking," he said. There was no response.

He picked up a small rock and tossed it at the man, hitting him in the head. Holiday whirled, pistol in hand and fired. Amos White fired, and both men yelped. White felt the bullet rip through his left arm and saw Holiday's head explode in a shower of blood, brains, and bone.

"I'm in a pickle now," Amos White said, trying to get his neckerchief tied around his bleeding arm. "Bone's broke for sure, got a dead man to drag out to the road, and gotta find my horse. Damn that hurts," he almost cried out, tying the rag as tight as he could with just one hand and a set of fine teeth.

He felt the bones crunch together as he pulled the knot down, knew the rag was already soaked with his blood. "Gotta get back to town," he said, moving slowly through the brush and rocks. "Need help," he almost whispered.

It took him until he was out on the road with his horse to realize that Corcoran wasn't with him. Didn't follow him out of the bank. "Damn, damn, damn," he said, fighting his way into the saddle. His shot and broken arm completely useless. He couldn't get Holiday's body onto his horse so left it by the side of the road. He was leading the other horse and started on the journey back to Eureka. "Nice and steady, big boy. I'm losing a lot of blood."

Corcoran's foot was in bad shape and he was in considerable pain as he tried to move out of the bank. He made it to the door and was hanging on to it when Sandy McAuliff came hobbling up. "So, got yourself all shot-up, eh? Well, come on, use me as a crutch. We got work to do. Young Amos is chasing Holiday. You and Lindstrom are both wounded."

"Go after him, Sandy. Follow their trail. We can't lose that boy and he'll need help. Tell Lindstrom to get Betty Cord over here to tend to us. Go, Sandy."

McAuliff didn't argue for a second. Amos White

had been his friend for years, and it was he who got the boy into this mess in the first place. *I helped grow that boy up after his father lost their ranch. Helen Whipple's gonna get her man.* He found Lindstrom and sent him after Betty Cord, found his horse, and began the long ride to find Amos. "Lindstrom said he was riding north, but going cross country. I'll take the road."

He was still weak from his epic battle with the blizzard in the Cortez Range and rode at a solid trot down out of the canyon, taking the road north to Palisade. He couldn't get the fear of Amos being killed, or seriously wounded. "Miss Helen ain't gonna like this. Not one bit."

He turned north to follow the railroad tracks along a fairly flat and wide road. He rode at a comfortable lope for the first half hour and then down to a walk to let the horse blow. The air was bitter cold without a cloud to be seen and no wind. Sandy McAuliff didn't consider himself an old man despite the number of years that had passed, but with his recent serious head injury, he knew he couldn't keep up a strong pace for long. He would give out long before his horse.

He saw where Holiday and Amos had jumped the culvert and come onto the roadway and put his horse back into a gentle lope. It was another half hour before he found Amos White slumped in the saddle, his horse slowly walking back toward town. "Amos," he called out, racing up to the boy.

"Amos. Wake up, boy." He rode up alongside, shook the big man hard, saw the bloody rag tied around the broken arm, and shook him again. Amos White sat bolt upright, looked around quickly, and gave the old tracker about half a smile.

"Afraid I was in heaven," he laughed. "Guess I went the other way."

"Shush, now," Sandy laughed. "Can you ride at a lope or hard trot? We got to get you back in town right away."

"I'll try, Sandy. Weak," he muttered, pushing his horse into a solid trot. Making their circles, keeping track of the cattle, buckaroos often make fifty or sixty miles a day at a trot, but seldom with a gunshot wound and broken bones. "Stay close, Sandy. I've lost a lot of blood. I ain't never felt this weak."

"We're about ten miles out, Amos. It's gonna be hard, and best if we don't stop. What happened between you and Holiday?"

Amos told him the story and McAuliff whooped some. "You did the right thing not walking right up on that bastard, but he was fast, wasn't he. Betty Cord is taking care of Terrence and Ed. Corcoran got his foot busted up bad and Lindstrom was hit as well."

The talk became one sided and after about ten minutes McAuliff had to catch Amos White before he fell from the saddle. "Oh, damn me," he said, trying to keep the big man in the saddle and bring both horses to a stop. "Damn, damn, damn," he said over and over, getting the horses off the road, Amos out of the saddle without hurting him even more, and getting the horses tied off.

McAuliff felt every year, was winded as he laid Amos out in an area of mixed grass and mud. He laid the big man on top of his bedroll, and used Amos's bedroll to cover him. "This is terrible," he muttered, trying to catch his breath. "Gotta get a fire going. Gotta save that boy."

After so many years guiding and tracking for the army, he was moving by instinct, visions of those days etched in his brain. McAuliff gathered some broken pine limbs, sage brush, and grass, and got a good fire going. "Gotta keep you warm, boy." He went through Amos's saddlebags and found a beat up and badly dented coffee pot and some beans, knew he didn't have any, and got a pot started.

"Well, let's see what I can do about this arm. You have been bleeding heavy for sure." Trying to tie off a bandage on a bleeding wound with just one hand is difficult at best and Sandy saw that White's efforts were far short of doing their job. "You needed that extra hand, Amos." He had to chuckle at the mess the deputy had made. "Well, you got it now, boy." He put pressure on the wound and got the bleeding stopped. It was difficult getting a splint on the broken bones, mostly because of the bullet wound, but he did get it stabilized.

Wrapped in a clean rag that once was one of Amos's shirt tails, McAuliff took the time to stoke up the fire and worry about how to get Amos White back to town alive. "Must be close to zero out here. We can't stay, gotta move, gotta keep him awake." How would he do that? Questions blazed in his head. How could he lift that big man into the saddle? How could he keep him there? "I can't do this. I ain't gonna let this boy die, but I can't do this," he was almost crying, fully understanding just how old and weak he was.

Despite the bright sun it was bitter cold. McAuliff knew it was below zero, and it penetrated layers of clothing. McAuliff felt the chill, knew an injured man would be even more affected. He spent years guiding the army in the northern Rockies, in the Black Hills of western Dakota Territory, in blizzards and freezing cold, and knew he and Amos White would not survive a night without some kind of protection and food.

"Can't leave him and he'll die if I just stay. I ain't

strong enough to get him in the saddle and he ain't strong enough to stay there. Well, just damn me," he snarled. He had a tin cup of coffee in hand when Amos White asked for some. "Didn't know you were back with us, Amos. Got you patched up some." He gave him his cup and went to the horses to find another cup. "How we gonna get you back to town?"

"I'm fine," White said. He drank most of the coffee and pulled the bedroll off. Sitting up, McAuliff saw Amos's eyes roll back, White dropped the tin cup, and fell back onto the bottom bedroll, unconscious.

"Guess you're not," McAuliff whispered, covering him up. The old army scout sat on the ground in front of the fire, tears running down his cheeks. "I can't get you back, son. I can't."

CHAPTER TWENTY-THREE

"There's something wrong, Ed, and there's nothing either one of us can do about it." Corcoran was on a bed, his deputy Ed Lindstrom on one next to him. His foot was twice its normal size, bandaged with blood showing through. Doc Weatherford was working on Lindstrom.

"Neither one of you boys is going anywhere," the cranky old doctor growled.

"Somebody has to, Doc. Sandy McAuliff is out chasing down Amos White and should have been back hours ago. I've got to get a posse put together and go for them."

"You're not moving, Corcoran," Weatherford said again. "And neither is Lindstrom."

"Get Betty Cord for me," Corcoran said. "Please Doc, you know very well that McAuliff isn't that strong and somebody out there might be hurt bad. Please."

Weatherford had a lot of respect for McAuliff, had patched him up many times, and knew there was a serious threat. He loved being a cantankerous old devil but there was a time and a place for that. "I'll get her," he said. "Probably at the Bonanaza Club."

"No," Lindstrom said. "She's at Henry Carter's store."

The doctor had Betty back in minutes. Corcoran laid out the problem as quickly as he could. "McAuliff should have been back hours ago. Something's wrong and a search needs to start right away. It'll be dark in a couple of hours, Betty. Neither White nor McAuliff is fitted out to spend a night in this cold. Find Jimmy Henderson and get a posse organized. Hurry."

"Tell 'em to take the road north," Lindstrom said. "That was the direction Holiday took."

She bent down and kissed Corcoran right in front of everyone and ran out the door. "You do have a way, Corcoran," Lindstrom laughed. Corcoran just laid back on the pillow with a grin spread across his craggy face. Inside, his heart was beating, fear for his two favorite people raging. *I hope I didn't send those two out to their ends. I'm hung up, the sheriff is hung up, my deputy is bedside with me, and those two are out in this terrible weather.*

Jimmy Henderson heard Betty's story and walked up to the bar, banging his pistol grip to get everyone's attention. "Sheriff Corcoran got shot in that failed bank robbery this morning and Deputy Amos White is chasing the killer Jonas Holiday. Sandy McAuliff is following. Corcoran feels something is wrong, that we should have heard from them before now, and he can't ride.

"I need five good men to ride with me to find Amos White and Sandy McAuliff. I'm riding out in ten minutes," he said. He drank down a shot of whiskey, looked at barman Jack Munson. "Give me a bottle to take with us."

He rode up in front of the Bonanza Club and found ten mounted men ready to ride. "We go at a lope gentlemen. We're off to save these men, not kill our horses," and he turned his black stud, leading the posse down out of the canyon.

The blacksmith, George Acres rode alongside. "As cold as it is, Jimmy, those people could be in trouble if somebody's hurt."

"I think that's what Corcoran's worried about. That White kid is a strong one. He's going to marry Helen Whipple and take over Hank's ranch." Henderson chuckled. "Hank's the winner and Corcoran's losing a good deputy."

"If Sandy McAuliff and Amos White are chasing that bastard Holiday, you can bet Holiday's gonna be the loser. White already shot him once."

"Would have been for the best if he'd killed the man," Henderson said. "McAuliff's the one I'm worried about. He should have died on the last ride he made, and it was only because of Amos White that he's alive today. We gotta find those men, George. No matter what, we gotta find those men."

The sun was moving toward the western horizon fast and McAuliff was getting more and more worried. Amos would come to for a few minutes, then lapse back. The cold was getting more intense as the afternoon wore on. "I am not going to lose this man," McAuliff said. He had the fire burning hot, but they had no food, no other protection than the two bedrolls and the two saddle blankets. The old guide had just enough water left to make one more pot of coffee.

Each time the old tracker went out to fetch sage and broken limbs for the fire he seemed weaker. The loads were smaller each time, and McAuliff knew the end couldn't be too far off. He would run out of energy to get wood and the fire would die, and when that happened, they would die.

"I've got to get those horses saddled, get that big

man in the saddle, and ride to town. I have to," he said. The fact that he was older than he admitted, weaker than he told anyone, and still suffered massive headaches, was catching up to McAuliff. "Ive faced worse," he tried to chuckle. He had his pipestem half eaten, but still working, and put a coal to the tobacco. "But I had an army patrol with me in those days."

He tried to get Amos White to sit up, and White gave it everything. He was sitting, but the world was spinning when he opened his eyes. "Whoa, Sandy. Not too fast now. It's cold." He tried to pull the blanket around his shoulders and almost toppled over. McAuliff caught him, got him steadied.

"We got to make a run for it, Amos. Gonna freeze us solid if we stay. I'm as weak as you are, but I'm not gonna let you die, boy. You got a wonderful life in front of you. You got Helen and your kids to think about."

"Kids! We ain't got no kids. What are you talking about?"

"You're gonna have, but I gotta get you back to town so you will have." He threw some more wood on the fire. His stack of torn out sage brush was getting smaller by the hour. "Let's see if we can get you to your feet. If we can do that, we'll get you in the saddle and ride, boy. Ride."

Sandy McAuliff didn't weigh one hundred forty

pounds at best, was weak from his injury, and was trying to get a man who weighed nearly two hundred pounds, equally weak, to his feet. "I can't do it, Sandy. No balance. Everything's spinning," and he fell back onto the bedroll, almost unconscious. McAuliff fell to the ground next to him, crying, almost sobbing.

"I can't either, boy. I'm so sorry." He held onto Amos's shoulder, saying he was sorry over and over. Neither one of the men heard the whoops and hollers from half a mile down the road.

"That's a fire burning, Acres," Henderson hollered out, pointing at what had to be a large campfire well down the road. "Let's ride," he shouted, spurring his stud. The herd thundered to a stop in front of the fire. Henderson leaped out of the saddle and ran to where Sandy McAuliff sat with his arms around Amos White.

"Sandy," Henderson yelled, waking the old tracker. "You're alive, my God, man, you're alive. Come on men, get that fire up, get some coffee going, get some hot food for these two."

It was a scramble, almost out of control, and it was George Acres who took control. He had a few men gathering wood, one making coffee, and another getting fresh and smoked meat hot for everyone.

Amos White responded to the coffee and hot food,

and with several men pushing and shoving, was in the saddle as the sun went behind the mountains. They could feel the immediate drop in temperature. Two men rode, one on each side of Amos, all the way back. He was in and out of consciousness, often delirious, on the long slow ride. He responded to the hot food but lost a lot of it on the way back. He was in and out of consciousness, delirious, calling out for Helen, Sandy, even Corcoran.

Sandy McAuliff couldn't remember being as tired as he was. "Better keep an eye on me, Henderson. I was going to lose that boy," he said, so softly that Henderson wasn't sure he actually heard him. "Scared, Jimmy. I was so scared, so cold, so weak. Don't ever let yourself get old. I couldn't do anything." He was sitting straight up in the saddle but Henderson knew the man was half delirious, simply riding from instinct.

"Couldn't do anything? My God, man, you saved that boy's life. Saved your own, too."

He's from a different time, that old man. Served in the original Indian wars, guided and tracked where only Indians and animals had been before. Amos White is alive because he knew what to do and did it. Jimmy Henderson had great admiration for men and women who took it upon themselves to do what needed to be done. *That's probably why I have such admiration for men like Terrence Corcoran.*

"let's pick it up, men," Henderson yelled out. "These are heroes we're bringing back. Drinks are on the house when we get these gentlemen home safe." From a walk to a solid trot, the group rode strong to Eureka.

George Acres rode ahead to alert Doc Weatherford, and it was almost a party atmosphere when the posse arrived back in town. It was cold, dark, and half the town was on the street cheering their welcome back.

Amos White held onto Jimmy Henderson with both hands as the saloon keeper helped him into Doc's house. "Into bed with you," Henderson said, easing the young deputy down. George Acres helped McAuliff out of the saddle and walked him into the house.

"About time you got back," Corcoran chuckled, seeing White's smiling face. "I'm gonna miss you, Amos."

"I got him," the almost retired deputy smiled and closed his eyes. He was warm and fast asleep.

Yes, you did and Sandy got you. Two best friends I've ever had, losing one to age and the other to love. Just, damn me and doggone it.

Doc Weatherford worked for hours on White's wound and broken bone, forced Sandy McAuliff to take a sleeping potion, and called it a night sometime around midnight. He was up tending the fires, making coffee, and getting ready to check on his patients by five the next morning. "For a sleepy little mining camp, this place sure makes me tired," he grumbled.

Amos White wakened when Weatherford came into his room. "Where am I?" He looked around, wide-eyed and spotted the doctor. "Doc? What happened?"

"You awake enough to have some coffee? Good. Enjoy this while I get Corcoran in here, and he'll ask the questions while I change your bandages." He was back in a couple of minutes trailing a limping Terrence Corcoran. "You two talk, I'll work."

"You got him, Amos. Good work. Do you remember how it went down?"

"Vividly," Amos White said. Waking up in a strange bed, in a room he didn't recognize threw him off for a couple of minutes, but he was awake now, ready to tell his story. "I am one weak child," he coughed.

"You're lucky to be alive, boy. Sandy McAuliff saw to that. Quit moving around so I can get these bones back where they belong." Weatherford was gentle as a kitten working on his patients, but grouchy in demeanor all the time. He relished being grouchy and some say he even practiced when no one was around.

White spent the next few minutes detailing the chase and the kill. "I've always walked up to a downed deer or elk and lightly touched my rifle barrel to an eye to see if the animal was fully dead. I threw a rock at

Holiday. I'd be dead if I'd tried the eye trick. He was so fast, Corcoran."

"Yeah, and so were you, Pard. So were you. Doc's got me fixed up with a walking crutch, and I know Ed Connor is gonna want to hear all about this. Don't go anywhere. I'll be back." *I bet that boy don't even know how to spell fear. I'm glad for him that Helen Whipple came along but I sure wish she hadn't.*

Amos White was laughing right out as Corcoran walked out. "Don't go anywhere, he said," laughing at the doctor. "How bad is my arm, Doc? I don't feel much pain."

"You ain't going anywhere and you will feel that pain, Amos. You will. I've got it set, but because of the wound, I can't put it in a cast. I've got splints tied on and will have to untie them to tend the wound daily. As soon as the wound is partly healed, I can put your arm in a cast. Until then, don't do anything. Just limited movement for the next several days."

"As tired as I feel, I'm taking you up on that." Loss of blood and intense cold had sucked the energy right out of Amos White, and, while he was aware that Weatherford was working on him, his mind was on Helen, the Rocking W, and a lifetime of chasing cows. "Before you do anything, Doc, how is Sandy? He found me, but it's kinda blurry after that."

"You're alive because of that old man, Amos. He did everything right."

Betty Cord came in with a tray full of food and a pot of coffee. She was followed by Sandy McAuliff. "I thought it was all over, Amos. I really did." He looked at Betty, then Doc Weatherford. "Thank you, Betty, for putting Jimmy Henderson on our trail. We'd a been dead for sure in another couple of hours. He gonna be okay, Doc?"

"Just look at his eyes and ask that question, McAuliff. He's fine now, thanks to you. Keeping him warm and tending that wound properly, saved that arm. He's lucky to have a friend like you."

"I'd be dead if wasn't for him, Doc. He pulled me through the Cortez blizzard. I owe him my life."

Doc saw two very similar men separated by half a century. *I can't imagine what it would be like if these two were the same age riding together. Twins is what I'm looking at. Twin Titans, for God's sake, both owing the other their lives.* He was wearing a smile, shaking his head back and forth. "Both of you need a good rest."

"Are you telling me there isn't one single deputy on duty in my town?" Ed Connor was sitting straight up, glaring at Corcoran. "Not one?"

"Not even a sheriff," Corcoran chuckled. "You're in

a cast, my foot's all busted up, Lindstrom's suffering from a gunshot wound as is Amos White, and even our jailer, Sandy McAuliff is in bed. Yup, the whole department's out of commission. Aren't you glad you turned everything over to me?"

Maryann Soto grabbed the coffee pot before Connor could throw it at Corcoran, sure as hell. Then the humor of the situation hit him too. All three were laughing loud, uproariously, when Peter Bridges walked in.

"Interrupting, am I?" He asked. "Wanted to tell you how pleased I am. Corcoran, you did a fine job breaking up that gang and stopping the robbery."

"He did a fine job wrecking the sheriff's office, too," Connor said. "I've got to get back on my feet and soon. The whole town's in danger if I let Corcoran stay on as acting sheriff for much longer."

There was general laughter from Maryanne, Corcoran, and the sheriff, and Peter Bridges, unaware of why, just stood in the doorway shaking his head. "I'll be at the bank if you need anything," he said.

"He better lock the doors." Maryanne said, bringing even more laughter.

"Seriously, Corcoran, what are you going to do about this? Sure as hell the bad element will realize there ain't no visible law."

"Aw, hell, Sheriff, I can still get around and so can Ed Lindstrom. I've got a buckaroo coming down from the Raine's place to take over White's position. Old Sonny Rafferty said he's a good man. No, I might have been joshing you some, Ed, but your town's gonna be safe."

CHAPTER TWENTY-FOUR

Betty Cord had two of the girls who worked for Jimmy Henderson helping as nurses, getting in Doc Weatherford's way as much as possible. She was still trying to run Henry Carter's store, take care of his children and his mother, and the strain was showing. "I sure hope you never ask my help again, Terrence Corcoran. Did you send that wire to Toby Smith like I asked?"

"Yup. Day before yesterday. No answer back yet, of course. I know thank you isn't enough. You sure have a train load coming." Corcoran was at his desk in the office, his bandaged foot on a stool, sipping coffee laced with some brandy. Winter may have come early, but was sincere in its efforts. Another storm had brought another layer of snow to the little mining camp and the sound of axes chopping wood was continuous.

"I don't really want a full-time job taking care of the

Carter family, Terrence. The old lady can't take care of herself, the kids need a full-time parent, and I need to get my own business started." Betty was tired, not yet angry but working on it, and she wanted Corcoran to know he better come up with an answer.

"Carter's trial is this week and the chances are better than even that he'll be spending several years in prison. The trial shouldn't take anymore than a day or two," he said.

"What'll happen to those kids? His mother can't take care of herself, more or less those kids."

"The court will have to figure that out. Kids' mother is dead, father in prison, and only other relative unable to care for them. Adoption or orphan house, I guess. The court will surely close or sell the business. I don't know."

"I'm going to talk to the judge. That old lady needs to be in an old folk's home, but those kids need someone to love and care for them. And, I need a store for my seamstress work." She looked deep into his bright green eyes and saw her own sadness reflected. "Come with me to talk to the judge."

"Fill my cup with coffee and brandy, sit with me while I drink it, and I will. Of course, there may be some hugs and kisses thrown in. Incentive, you know." She cuffed him, gently, and got the coffee and brandy first.

"Thank you, Toby," Hank Whipple said. "Stay with us for supper. You can ride back to Palisade tomorrow."

"Thanks, Hank, but I better get back. I'll make it before sunset if I try. Say hello to Esmeralda and Helen." It was a long ride from Palisade to the Rocking W and back, but Toby Smith was the only deputy left in the little mining town since the death of Jenkins.

Hank took the telegram into the house and called his wife and daughter into the kitchen. "Got some news on Amos White for you," he said.

"Finally," Helen said, taking the wire. She sat down at the table and unfolded the sheet to read it. "Oh, my God," she cried. "He's been shot. He's hurt, Papa. We've got to go, he needs me. Oh ... "

Whipple took the letter and read it, handed it to Esmeralda, and sat down at the table. "We'll take the buggy to Blackburn and catch the train south tomorrow morning. Let's pack for several days, Mama." He walked out of the warm kitchen to tell his winter crew that they would be alone for a week.

Hank Whipple was that kind of man. In his mind, Amos White was already a member of the family and was hurt. It was the family's responsibility to take care of him. When White came to him to ask for Helen's hand, the bond was made. Now, it was Whipple's responsibility to take care of his new son.

Esmeralda had Helen in her arms, the girl crying hard. "I knew this would happen, that he would die before we could get married."

"He didn't die, honey. A man has responsibilities that are different than ours, and your man is special. He will always have you as his number one priority, just as he has his job right now. He promised you that as soon as he found his replacement he would come to you. Well, you have to go to him. This time, he needs you."

The train ride through the Diamond Valley was beautiful, fresh snow hanging from the trees, a few flurries still flailing about in places, and a carpet of white covering the land. Helen only saw the beauty through wet eyes, saw horrible pictures of Amos White in bandages, unable to walk or talk, and cried most of the way.

Betty Cord and Jimmy Henderson had a buggy and were waiting for the Whipple's. "Must have been a nice trip down," Henderson said. Hank nodded.

"Saw heavy snow, which means good water cone spring. Faced with crying women, though ain't the best way to travel. Got a place for us?" Whipple asked.

The ride into town was fast. "I'll take you to Doc

Weatherford's and then we'll get your luggage settled in the hotel. I've arranged a large suite for you."

"Why don't we just drop Helen off at Weatherford's. Esmeralda and I will go on to the hotel with you and Miss Ford." Hank knew he and Esmeralda would just be in the way at the doctor's. "I'm sure those two will want to be alone."

Betty chuckled. "Every other thought has been on Helen. None on his wounds. He's mostly afraid that you'll be angry because he was still wearing a badge."

"Afraid, not angry," Helen whispered. "Was he hurt terribly bad?"

"He was shot in the arm and suffered a broken bone because of it. It was the ordeal afterward that sapped his energy. It was below zero and he had lost a lot of blood, but a warm bed, plenty of hot food, and he's like a young wolf right now, full of it, and ready to get out and do something. He's gonna be fine, Helen."

She was tentative, walking down the corridor to Amos's room, and almost tiptoed in. As soon as she saw him, she ran to the bed and flung herself on him. "Amos," she said, covering his face with kisses. "I was so scared."

He held her tight, ran his hands up and down her back, felt giddy and weak. "I'm fine, lovely lady, just fine. Doc says I'll be up and walking tomorrow or the next day. Maybe even today if I get more hugs from you."

"You'll get about a hundred years of hugs, Mr. White. Mama and Papa are here, too. We have rooms at the Bonanza. Can you come home with us? With me?" She blushed, kissed him quick, hid her face, looked up and kissed him again.

Amos was laughing hard for the first time in weeks and let himself just lie back and look into Helen's eyes. "I think we should get married before we leave town. I want Sandy McAuliff to stand with me."

"I've never heard more perfect words, Amos. Yes, we should as soon as the doctor says you can get out of bed. Tomorrow," she squealed, throwing her self at him again. He winced from the pain but kept her tight in his arms. The cast only got in the way a couple of times. "I've got to tell mama and daddy."

It was a festive wedding for the Whipple family but the day was far from festive for the Carter family. District Judge Porter Trumble sent Henry Carter to the Carson City State Prison for ten years, ruled his mother unable to care for herself and sent her to an old folk's home near Reno, and the children to an orphanage in Elko. Betty Cord had tears running down her cheeks but knew there was nothing she could do about it.

"All of this because Henry Carter was just a stupid and naive man? His children now homeless, his mother shucked under the covers somewhere? It just isn't right, Terrence Corcoran, but there isn't anything that can be done about it."

"Several families in town are discussing whether or not they can take Carter's children in. It might end well, yet," Corcoran said. "The word stupid fits more than just naive. The man never thought out a problem or saw what he was doing. Can't fix stupidity, darlin'."

"Welcome to the Whipple clan, Amos. I had a chat with Corcoran last night and he has a young buckaroo from the Raines outfit coming in as the new deputy, so you are free to come home and take up your responsibilities on the ranch."

"I was worried about that, Hank. Doc wants me to keep this cast on for another several weeks, but I'll be good as new well before spring calving. I have a large wagon from George Acres and a fine team. Helen and I will pack my stuff and ride back to the ranch."

"Good. That will give you children time to be alone. Esmeralda and I will leave on the morning train, then. You're a good man, Amos White. I'm proud to call you son."

Amos made his way to the sheriff's office to find

Corcoran. "Mixed up feelings, Sheriff." he said, finding Corcoran with McAuliff. "Don't want to say goodbye but want to also. These last several weeks have been the most exciting of my life."

"Too damn exciting for my blood," McAuliff laughed. "You saved my life, boy. I'll never forget you."

"Well, you made up for it saving mine," Amos said. "What's your real name? I know it isn't Sandy."

"No, lad, it isn't Sandy. My family is traditional Gaelic, and they named me Aonghus, most often pronounced Angus. My father wore his kilts proper, you know, as I do on special occasions."

Corcoran was laughing loud by this time. "He means, Amos, without benefit of underwear."

"Tradition is just as important as personal responsibility," McAuliff said, rather stiffly, bringing even more laughter. "Humph," the old tracker pretended to fume.

They shook hands all around, promised to visit back and forth regularly, and Amos White, no longer a deputy, went to his house to help Helen pack for the trip north. "I'd like to name our first boy Angus," he said. "That's Sandy's real name."

"And the second boy would be Terrence, I suppose?" Helen chuckled.

"Wonderful idea," he said. They spent as much time hugging and kissing as they did packing and it wasn't until late the next morning that they rode through town and down the canyon to the main road north.

"I chased Holliday on this road, Helen. I'll show you where everything took place as we ride along."

"I'd rather you didn't," she whispered. "I just want to hang on to you and dream about us raising children, cows, and horses." It was a pleasant journey with a lot of laughter.

Jimmy Henderson bought the Carter store and building and leased it to Betty Cord who kept the dry goods portion and added her seamstress business, which became an instant success.

There was little crime in Eureka over the next few weeks and Ed Connor was able to come to the office a few days each week, Ed Lindstom's leg healed up quickly, and Terrence Corcoran found he could get a boot on after several weeks. "It's nice to have my office back, Corcoran. Remind me not to get injured again. The county can't afford you being sheriff. By the way, Peter Bridges says it isn't necessary to give those keys back. He changed all the locks.

"See? Even he fears what damage you might cause if you got in the bank one night." Connor laughed right out and poured some brandy in his tin cup. "Johnny Lewis will be escorted to the Carson City Prison as soon as his guards get here. Like Carter, they'll take him by train. Is he any danger to try to escape?"

"Too damn dumb, Ed. Glad you're back," Corcoran said. He reached across the desk for the brandy bottle and filled his tin cup. "And your brandy."

"Gonna be strange around this old town without Colonel Cornell telling impossible tales. I guess Bridges will be happy knowing the old loud-mouth won't be telling everybody how to rob that bank." Ed Lindstrom said.

"This entire runaway freight train of events all because of Colonel Buford S. Cornell and his blow-hard lies." Corcoran sat back, sipped his brandy laden coffee, and shook his head slowly.

"Any Paper come in on anyone we should be looking for?" Connor poured another cup of brandy.

"Only thing I'm looking for is a long cold winter, sitting in front of a blazing fire, eating steak and beans," Corcoran said.

"Amen to that," Connor said.

A LOOK AT EZEKIEL'S JOURNEY BY JOHNNY GUNN

His life is shattered, his wife, his children dead. A lesser man might just give it up; but Ezekiel Hawthorne isn't a quitter. While thousands head to the California gold fields in wagons, Ezekiel loads his mule and embarks on an amazing venture across the continent alone, bound for the good soils and abundant waters of Oregon. Savages, tornadoes, and a lack of knowledge don't slow the man down a bit. It's a beautiful half-Shoshone woman who has the biggest impact on Ezekiel's new life.

AVAILABLE NOW ON AMAZON

ABOUT THE AUTHOR

Reno, Nevada novelist, Johnny Gunn, is retired from a long career in journalism. He has worked in print, broadcast, and Internet, including a stint as publisher and editor of the Virginia City Legend. These days, Gunn spends most of his time writing novel length fiction, concentrating on the western genre. Or, you can find him down by the Truckee River with a fly rod in hand.

https://wolfpackpublishing.com/johnny-gunn/